THE
FINAL
SEED

A NOVEL

'Unmarked Only'

Eric Alan Soldal

The Final Seed:
"He who Endures to the End Shall be Saved"
Copyright © 2023 Eric Alan Soldahl
Dovestar Publishing International
7149 Highway 11, Box #42 Sunset, SC 29685-9998
ISBN- 978-1-7356254-2-3
ISBN- 17356254 23

Published in the United States of America. 2023. 1st Edition

Chapter 1

"And in thy Seed shall all the nations be blessed; because thou hast obeyed my voice." Genesis 22:18

To Ben, it seemed as if the entire world had become mad with fear. Considering himself to be a rationally minded sort of man, this was a logical conclusion. Everywhere, people had holed up in their dwellings with eyes transfixed on televisions or computers, waiting for the next catastrophic scene of this new plague to unfold.

For most, it was almost sport to witness, from the comforts of home, a play-by-play action of what was termed a deadly Asian Coronavirus sweeping the world. The origins of which Ben held suspect when it was first reported to come from a "Bat Soup," sold in an outdoor Chinese marketplace.

As Ben drove home from work late that evening, he could not help but be amused after spotting a colleague at his university, wearing a mask; alone, in a convertible.

Ben's position as *Director of Genetics Lab,* at the campus facility, gave him access to much information in this matter. Most of it appeared to be contrary to the narrative. His team had poured over government documents and peer reviewed studies for accuracy and truth.

Pulling into the driveway, he could not wait to embrace his wife, Sara. As usual, her opening of their front green door came with perfect timing. Always welcome when arms were laden with stacks of research materials. Sara leaned over the
mound of paperwork for her kiss.

"Right on schedule," Ben smiled, "I'm so thankful there's someone left in the world who isn't afraid of catching a cold, or something."

"I was the only one without a mask at the women's prayer meeting today," she nodded confidently. "Only half of them showed up. All talking at once and not much prayer."

"This devil of a disease will divide," Ben raised a brow.

"Those in the choir argued over having everyone wear masks while they are singing!" Sara followed Ben to their back office in their modern mountain home. He neatly set the folders and electronics on a circular teak desk. Then with anticipation she asked, "Have you been finding out any more about all this, Ben?"

"First of all, more may come from prayer than anything else. Everywhere we search there is misleading information and missing documentation. It's buried or wiped clean off the servers. If we have discovered anything at all—a massive cover-up is going on."

"How so, Ben?

"The Emergency Health directive gives total immunity and power to these quasi-Government agencies and Executive branch. They appear to be controlled by un-elected officials and those who will benefit. They're promoting a narrative of fear and sickness."

"And the entire media is playing along with it," Sara shook her head while switching off the TV. "They're brainwashing everyone. It's late, how would you like dinner served in bed?"

"Sounds enticing." Ben turned on some peaceful piano music. "Best news I've heard all day."

The following morning, being Saturday, the couple relaxed for their usual, *Sabbath day*, as they often referred to it.

Ever since returning from the Holy Land in Israel, they were inspired to take this time away from work. To soak into time with God and each other. In the *Promised Land*, it was a time from Friday at sunset to Saturday evening when all activity ceased.

"This is my favorite day of the week," Sara would say.

"And no dishes to wash," Ben laughed.

They would listen to music, pray and read the scriptures together, take a waterfall hike, or in summer swim in the nearby rushing waters.

"A little gardening must be o.k. with God," Sara once mentioned, *"He walks with me and He talks with me,"* she sang a line joyfully from an old Hymn. Sara handed Ben a cup of Earl Grey Tea and recalled, "We better not forget our dinner tonight at the Mexican restaurant for the returning Missionaries."

"Seems optimistic with all of the lockdowns going on," Ben surmised.

"Well, it was planned a while ago."

"I'm sure there are many Missionaries being called home, or getting kicked out of these fearful countries now." Ben gazed up at the sky covered in a dreary white haze. It was brisk so he was thankful for the flannel shirt sent by his sister; a late January birthday present. Paying no attention to the whistling of the wind, he reclined on a dew-covered chaise lounge. "I just recalled a vivid dream from last night."

"What was it, Ben?" Sara was often intuitive.

"There was a man dressed all in white standing on the far bank of a wide river...he was motioning for me to come across. That's the whole dream."

"Maybe there's a connection to our Missionary dinner tonight," she considered.

The evening Missions dinner seemed filled with more fearful folks, muttering through masks. A few even kept them on while sitting for the Mexican fare of tacos and fajitas. *Must be messy eating with a mask on*, Ben mused. Reports were given through dinner on the trials with checkpoints, pat-downs and searches at the airports. Forceful police and security in Asia, India, or South America. There was trouble with U.S. Homeland Security upon arrival, with long waits and little appointed staff. The panic with lockdowns proliferated worldwide. Tests were required upon entry.

"Where is your faith over fear?" one exasperated young pastor asked the lukewarm group, who seemed more concerned over the toppings for their spicy tacos.

"Let's pray they get this thing under control," the senior pastor aired.

"For starters, this *'thing'* didn't come from a 'Bat Soup,'" Sara spoke out abruptly. "As you may know my husband is a medical researcher," she explained.

Ben chimed in, "Research leads us to question the mainstream narrative. Widescale testing will quickly lead to mass inoculations, without question, if we are not careful."

"Yes, but trust the doctors," was the consensus. "God made doctors too, you know," one missionary wife intervened.

On the drive home Sara lamented further, "I can't take it—why is everyone so blind and not questioning everything?"

At home, Ben opened his Bible to Thessalonians. "I found a verse that may explain what's going on."

Handing his old King James Bible to Sara, she read aloud, *"And for this reason God shall send them a strong delusion, that they should believe a lie—they received not the love of the truth that they might be saved."*

"Maybe the reason people are so deluded now is because they don't really want the truth," Ben suggested.

"Cognitive dissonance," Sara nudged him. "When people can't handle the truth, they stay in their comfortable denial."

"Your psychology degree to the rescue."

"When we take our next missionary trip, let's go without all the regulations and just share about Jesus," she smiled.

"The one couple said they spent most of their time in Beijing doing paperwork, for the 501 c3 church compliance."

Early Monday morning, while driving to work, Ben received a call from his nephew. In his thirties, Marshal was a senior programmer, working for one of the richest men in the world.

Two years earlier, they had attended his nephew's memorable wedding in Bellevue, Washington. A carnival atmosphere replete with arcades, life-size games and the latest tech gadgets.

Late that evening, Marshal's wealthy company owner, walked briskly past them with a large security guard. Out of curiosity, they had followed the infamous Billy Bates, into his palatial emerald glass high-rise office building.

The art-deco crystal light fixture extended several floors. "Poor taste," Sara had commented at the time.

On the thirteenth floor, an older black security guard spotted them and rushed over to intercede, "Didn't know I could still move so fast," his broad smile flashed bright.

After a brief exchange with Sara mentioning the wedding, the guard spoke in a hush, "Look, I've seen things—whatever you do, never, never, *NEVER*, trust that man..."

Now on the phone Marshal rattled off in a rapid staccato:

"Uncle Ben, since you seem to be the only sane member of our family, with this viral mess going on, I'm calling you on the low down. With your type of research work I'm wondering if you can tell me why they have us working overtime on a crypto currency technology program to place coding on biological matter?" Ben's mind pondered quickly.

"Are you saying the code you are writing is designed to alter the cells of humans for tracking finances?" Ben asked back.

"Worse than that, I think. Our division is doing the crypto, but its application is given via injections. Its under the guise of stopping infections, but will alter a person with an operating system somehow—I'm not privy to how all that will work."

Pausing to gather in more data, Ben carefully responded, "Listen Marshal, you are the truth-teller in our family. I know

you sense this is huge. Anyone's first instinct is to have you run from that place. When your dad was assembling some of the first microcomputers, Bates was always snooping around. He mentioned Jobs and Woz never trusted him. They all thought he was a shady character.

Your Aunt Sara recently discovered that Billy Bates' own Dad was the chief legal counsel for Planned Parenthood. His mom was with IBM, a company that helped the Nazi's track Jews during the second World War. A born depopulationist."

"One other thing, Uncle Ben, they're working with MIT and a patent is pending for this tech. Some here are wondering why the patent number is so blatantly suspect."

"What is it?"

"The working patent number is: NWO2020-060606.

After some of our team spoke up, they're dropping the 'N.'

"Why is the 'N' such a concern?" Ben asked.

"The 'N' was for *New* as in *New World Order*, and the 2020 is obvious because this is the year to be implemented. But it's the 060606 that I saw through right away..."

"How's that?"

"Well, in coding the zeros mean nothing, nada, they're for binary fill. So, I guess this really means '666,' right? Isn't that Biblical?"

"It's from the book of Revelation, called '*The Apocalypse*,' in many countries. If you still own a Bible, I suggest we both read the book of Revelation tonight. The devil is in the details."

Marshal let out a nervous sounding laugh, "Check this out; there is a substance in the MIT concoction that will light up when someone is scanned. They're calling it *'Luciferase,'* from a bio-luminescent hydra plankton creature."

"They will be able to monitor who takes it that way—disturbing how they are planning to *track* people."

On their usual evening walk together, Ben was more quiet than usual. Sara looped her arm through his, content to stroll in the crisp mountain air. The scent of three-needle pine permeated the pathway.

Drifting back to the telling conversation with his nephew, Ben recalled to himself how stoic Marshal had been when his dad died. *Jeremy was the eldest of Ben's brothers. He had taken one of the first computer companies public in record time. Marshal gravitated to mastering both hardware and software by the age of fifteen, garnering the attention of many in the industry; including Billy Bates.*

Ben's brother, Jeremy, riding the crest of the tech boom, expanded quickly with so much debt, that the company, Sunn Micro Systems, became a target. Apple and Steve Jobs, were also in a pinch and Bates seized on the moment. Apple repaid their loans, but Sunn Micro, as a subsidiary, was gobbled up by Bates. Jeremy mysteriously fell ill afterward, diagnosed with lead poisoning. His nephew, Marshal was part of the Sunn acquisition, feeling obligated to repay their family, so heavily invested in the company. After Jeremy's death, Marshal had become like a surrogate son to Ben. In a tug-of-war, Bates had a stronghold and knew how to manipulate the talent.

On the walk now, Ben broke the silence first. "Let's read Revelation together..."

"Sure—but what brought that on?" she wondered.

"It was the call with Marshal—the tribulation may be on the horizon. I asked him to read Revelation too."

"Well then, let's say some prayers that he will."

Chapter 2

"Now the parable is this, the Seed is the Word of God." Luke 8:11

That night, Ben ruffled the covers in disquieted sleep. Laying in the darkness, he considered these things happening so quickly. Sara breathed peacefully in slumber, providing some comfort. Earlier evening, his department head, Dr. Pidgeon, had called saying the University was closing temporarily due to the dreaded new plaque.

With access to the lab denied, how will we discover anything? Ben considered the motives. Although a private institution; *Why would the University be compromised like this? Who truly directed this closure?*

In the morning, Ben voiced his concerns over the lab shutting down on a call with his boss.

"Let's not get all fired up here," Dr. Pidgeon responded. "Labs are closing everywhere."

"How will the medical research community provide any independent oversight or assistance?" Ben gave an appeal.

"We will just have to trust their science." Pidgeon's response came too easily.

That's precisely the point, Ben wisely guarded his thoughts.

We can't trust them. Often, we expose them...

Over a late breakfast, he remembered the admonition to his nephew: *'Read Revelation.'* Later, Sara found him with eyes closed on the sofa with the Bible open to Chapter 14. "Taking a Bible snooze?" she whispered.

Springing upright, Ben asked, "Have you read this part in Revelation about the *Mark of the Beast* before?"

Sara sat down next to him propping up a brightly colored pillow she had embroidered and began reading aloud, *"And lo, a Lamb stood on mount Zion, and with Him a hundred and forty and four thousand, having His Father's name written in their foreheads."* Sara paused, "The Lamb is Jesus and these are the faithful when He returns, right?"

"Yes, I believe so," Ben confirmed.

Sara continued reading halfway through the chapter, then handing him Bible, "Your turn," she flashed a smile.

"And a third angel followed them saying with a loud voice, if any man worships the beast and his image, and receives his mark in their forehead, or in their hand." Ben pointed down at the tattered page, *"and he shall be tormented with fire and brimstone..."*

Sara grabbed his hand to stop the reading, "So they're tormented with fire and brimstone like in Sodom and Gomorrah?"

"Must be," Ben answered. "It goes on to repeat that those who take the Mark of the Beast, *'will have the smoke of their torment ascend up forever and ever and they will have no rest day nor night.'"*

"Quite a warning," Sara clutched his hand. "Count me out."

"Count me out, too. But we know the ones refusing to take it, will be persecuted."

He gazed longingly at his wife. "Let's trust the Lord."

"I'm glad you're home for a time, Ben," she comforted.

After a long walk together, Ben turned on the evening news. It was rare to watch television. A challenge to find any decent content, as in their youth. Every station now seemed a *puppet to the pandemia.* Changing the channels, it appeared their very content was in a stilted sync, showing the same reels of men in China wearing white hazmat suits. The chemicals they sprayed covered the skies, over deserted city streets, in stores, or apartment buildings—the men in protective suits often entering to enforce lockdowns. Each station repeatedly showed a young Asian man in a mall, dropping dead on the spot.

After dinner, one of Ben's colleagues from the Lab, called, "Have you been following this madness?" Charlie was exasperated, "I have been tracking this throughout the world without much sleep now—there's a pattern. Yesterday, all of the news outlets reported the same number of cases in each city. Today it's the same, except they have increased the number."

"That's statistically impossible," Ben quickly responded.

"Just a sham," Charlie offered, "There were '233 new cases' reported yesterday in every region and today it's six hundred and sixty-six. Every region gives the same findings; I bet tomorrow the numbers will quadruple again."

"A suckers bet, that one," Ben tried to lighten the call, "Even the newscasters wear masks!"

"Maybe they don't want you to see their lying lips."

Ben switched gears, "Listen, before closing our department down, I stumbled onto something." Although risky, he made arrangements to meet Charlie at the Lab the following night.

Sara reminisced while making a flower arrangement. It was a nice distraction from the order of the day. As a pre-school teacher, her hobbies came in handy. The closing of her classroom seemed premature, but she would not let herself become upset. The daughter of a medical doctor, she thought back to simpler times. Her dad, an Endocrinologist, was concerned for each one of his patients, often taking them off of prescribed drugs.

With an unassuming manner, he once sternly warned one of his wealthiest patients, "You will be dead within a year, if you don't stop the drinking." The man's wife had returned a year later to thank him with fresh baked cookies, saying he had saved their marriage; her husband had quit drinking.

She thought back to how she met Ben in the hospital elevator, while she was a pediatric volunteer one summer;

"Going my way?" he asked confidently.

She was attracted to Ben from the start. She looked forward to seeing him at the hospital daily. Like clockwork, he came at noon to visit his dad, recovering from colon surgery.

Ben first noticed Sara in the waiting room consoling others. Her skin glowed bright and he liked her long hair. "It's a cascade of many colors," he often tried to sound poetic. Ben was two years older, while she was yet to turn twenty.

He read medical journals while patiently waiting for his dad to stir awake. She pondered his intelligence and curiosity from the start. He had once caught a glimpse of her rocking babies to sleep in the maternity ward.

Sara was first to *break-the-ice* with conversation, while in the surgical waiting room, "Are you here for a loved one?" She had tried sounding sophisticated.

"My dad is in colon surgery," he responded. *Must be the worst opening line in history,* he worried at the time.

"Well, I hope you don't mind my asking. My dad is a doctor on rounds here. I lost my own mother to leukemia a few years ago." *Here his dad is in surgery and I tell him my mom die*d, she hoped it did not seem callous.

It did not deter Ben, who asked, "Maybe we can meet in the cafeteria on your break." Over the following weeks they met every noon, for lunch, and by the following year were married. Ben's dad acted as the minister at their wedding, with stage four cancer at the time, holding stoic throughout. He passed away shortly thereafter.

Sara's reminiscing ended when the flower arrangement was completed. She found Ben outside washing the car. Running to hug him she cooed, "Here's my soulmate!"

The next morning, Ben descended the stairs seeing his wife watering from the high deck, through the tall 'A frame.'

He admired her smart watering technique as the aerial spraying covered a lot of ground below.

Sara called up, "I wonder what my dad knows about all this."

Ben immediately found her cell and held the phone up for Sara, "Hi dad, what do you make of all this medical hysteria?"

Doctor Gill promptly responded with a serious tone, "I hope Ben is listening too."

"Yes, he's right here, dad."

"Hi Ben! Glad you're on the call. The medical community needs to move cautiously on this. Often, the FDA, CDC and other government agencies, overreact in these cases. They will all be vying for the research and grant money now. There's to be a push by the pharmaceuticals, but they always make us wary, don't they, Ben?" he asked rhetorically.

"Billy Bates practically own the World Health Organization now," Sara chimed in. "He wants to inoculate the whole world with an experimental mRNA gene altering therapy, Ben says."

"Well let's not jump to any conclusions at this point," the phone crackled as her father spoke. "But I will say that any doctor with half a brain knows that a virus mutates too quickly for a vaccine to be effective." Suddenly, the call dropped. Ben had carefully shied away from discussing too much with his father-in-law; he was highly intelligent, yet favored allopathic medicine, born of the Rockefeller dominated education system.

"I'm sure dad did not hang-up on us," Sara retorted. "I read that the Bates Foundation donated more money to the WHO than our federal government did last year."

Deep down, Ben held great respect for this man and their generation. Sara's dad had run the largest endocrine diagnostic center in the West for many years.

Tall and lanky at age 82, he still sang in the church choir until the recent lockdowns. He had been a devoted husband, supported charitable causes and walked eighteen holes of golf twice weekly.

"Still shooting better than I deserve and better than my age," Sara's dad spoke out.

From a medical standpoint Ben usually agreed with his father-in-law, although Ben researched more natural remedies and believed in a literal creation from the Genesis narrative in the Bible. Dad was ostensibly an evolutionist.

One time in a heated discussion on the golf course, Sara's dad had raised a club defiantly in his direction, after Ben had stated, "I believe it takes more faith to believe we came from an accidental explosion. "Did a one cell organism from pond scum, crawl out of the primordial ooze and become a chimp, an ape and then a man!?" It helped that his father-in-law deftly sank a fifty-foot putt on the next hole.

"What really struck me from the call with your dad, is his comment, *A virus mutates too quickly for a vaccine to ever be effective,*" Ben confided.

"And he said it with such conviction," Sara agreed.

That night it was Sara's turn assessing the gravity of the situation. While trying to fall asleep, she thought about how blessed they had been since giving up alcohol a decade earlier. *It gets easier as we go*, she realized. It seemed their love for each other had deepened since. It was rare when they disagreed on something. She thought about her plight in not having children. Countless hours had been spent in prayer and petition to the Lord, but now with the mid-century milestone looming about her age, the prospect of child bearing caused despair, on occasion.

Although having good intentions, friends and siblings often made matters worse, with comments such as, "Oh Sara, you're a pre-school teacher, you have more kids than any of us." Ben also tried consoling, reminding her of nieces, nephews, and how she filled his life completely. Yet she knew he had always desired a family.

And now there was this divide developing in the country. Those pushing masks and those opposed. *Was all of this leading to a divide over the coming injections?* Finally, Sara found slumber with a simple, silent prayer, *"Lord, forgive my mistrust, bless us indeed and keep us from the evil one..."*

At church the following morning, they were surprised to see the service was held in the parking lot. Everyone remained in their cars as the pastor spoke from the church steps talking over car radios! "Tune into 95.7 on your AM dial," a large sign read. Sara nudged Ben, who noticed the family in the car next to them all wore masks.

"This is a little macabre," Ben divulged. The songs and the message were unintelligible over the air. As they drove out of the parking lot there was a man in a double mask with a plastic shield. He held out an offering basket attached to a long pole. Ben recognized his friend and called out "Andy!"

The usher friend turned away in apparent embarrassment.

Monday morning found Ben heading out for groceries, before store shelves emptied, as was reportedly coming. Ben chuckled to himself, recalling news scenes showing people wrestling at the markets, over the last of the toilet paper.

Stopping at his favorite coffee shop, he was glad to find they were still open for business. A sign in the window read: *"Masks Required for Entry."* Ben, who was maskless, breezed by the young man standing at the door, holding the sanitizer gel for every patron. Hand sanitizer gel was in every public location, required for entry. *The owners of all the chemical companies must be promoting sanitizers to governments as a protocol,* he surmised.

The chemical companies who made *Roundup*, and other poisons, were now controlled by the pharmaceuticals. With a minimum of research, Ben had discovered the gels were an endocrine disruptor; potentially leading to auto-immune, and fertility disorders.

The younger workers all wore masks, but Ben spotted one older gentleman sitting in the corner flashing a smile in his direction. Drawing closer, Ben noticed he wore frameless glasses and was reading an old Bible.

Brushing aside his bushy beard, the man held up the giant book with hands almost as large, "Quite a treasure," he spoke out, "Found it just this morning in a second-hand store near Asheville. It's an original King James from the mid eighteen hundreds." The man paused and seemed to size up Ben standing in front of him. "Noticed you wear a wedding ring, any children?"

"No kids yet, but an amazing wife, of twenty-four years."

"Good to hear that these days. See you have a little salt and pepper on the roof," he elaborated, pointing at Ben's hair starting to grey. "Better get started on those kids—there's always adoption, you know..."

"I'm Ben," he responded, extending his hand.

"Call me Pastor A.J. We give handshakes and hugs where I come from. No fist-bumps allowed," he laughed jovially. "Why don't you grab some coffee and come join me for a bit."

A long thoughtful conversation ensued. They shared life-testimonies and solved all the problems of the world. Within an hour, a brotherly bond had formed. Both agreed mankind simply needed a Savior, named Jesus.

On the way home, Ben called his wife, "Hi hon, sorry I'm late, the grocery store refused my entry without a mask on. And I also met quite an interesting man at the coffee shop."

"What did you do?"

"I had some coffee and an amazing talk. A.J. is a pastor."

"I meant what did you do at the store about the mask?"

"Oh—appealing with logic, I asked the manager, 'How does someone purchase a mask here without entry?'"

"Did you let him know masks are unhealthy, harboring bacteria and don't work?" Sara suggested.

"Well, I did mention it was hazardous breathing in your own carbon dioxide. I ended up going to the Farmers Market. So nice to see those folks are not buying into the rhetoric."

The first signs of Spring began to appear by the road. "Wildflowers!" Ben called out over the car speaker phone. "The best news is we were invited to church by the pastor I met at *Heavenly Grounds* this morning. He's a former Green Beret. Maybe the last one around standing for Biblical truth."

Late that night, Ben met his co-worker at the University by the back entrance of their Lab. Charlie peeked out the door speaking almost imperceptibly,

"It's not good, Ben, we've had a break-in..."

Flipping the lights on to the outer office, Ben wondered why there were no security guards around. Oddly, the office alarm system had been deactivated. Inside, paperwork was strewn in disarray and file cabinets lay open. All the lab equipment seemed to be left intact for some reason.

Charlie handed Ben an envelope, "I found this taped to the mainframe computer." Ben's name was typed on the front.

He quickly folded and placed the white envelope in his front pants pocket. Charlie motioned for them to leave the same way they had come in—through the back stairwell. Ben suggested they depart quickly, before any security arrived.

"I wonder what Dr. Pidgeon, knows about all this," Charlie impugned, wary of their department chair. "He's jealous of your research project, Ben." They agreed Charlie would leave the break-in report anonymously.

Impulsively, opening the envelope in his driveway, Ben found a phone number. Below the number was a handwritten message on a bright green post-it-note. It read: *Please call immediately, millions of lives may be in your hands. Dr. Cole.*

There was an ominous quote included at the bottom:

"The spirits of darkness are going to inspire their human hosts, in whom they are dwelling, to find a vaccine that will drive all inclinations towards (God) and spirituality 'out' of people's souls." Rudolph Steiner, *from a Lecture in 1917*

Chapter 3

"He that received Seed into the good soil is he that heareth the Word and understands it," Matthew 13:23

At home, Ben discussed the evenings events with Sara, over a cup of tea. He told her about the break-in at the Lab and the envelope Charlie discovered with his name on it. The insistence to call a Dr. Cole, for saving *"millions of lives..."*

"The area code on the note is not listed anywhere."

"Well, its late now. Either someone is trying to give you their problem, or your expertise is really needed."

"Let's pray about it first," he started to yawn. "Will call this Dr. Cole in the morning, if so led."

In the morning, Ben considered the events from the previous night. Convicted at not reporting the break-in, he sent Charlie a follow-up text message: *Did you contact Dr. Pidgeon, or security at the University yet? What if we were spotted on a different camera?*

Hesitantly, Ben dialed the number given on the bright green note. A man with a deep voice answered, "Dr. Cole." His drawl sounded, '*cow-all*'...

"You left me a note at our University Lab?"

"Thank God you phoned—is this Ben—Ben Strickland?"

"Yes..."

"I have been following your research since the Epigenetics break-through at Duke. Your help is needed for this crisis.

A co-worker gave me your contact information last week. My background is also in medical research."

What followed was an in-depth plea for Ben to meet him in Raleigh, North Carolina. He admitted being heavily monitored with a top-level position in virology. There had been some leaks of his recent bio-tech and viral discoveries. After calling for a government investigation, Dr. Cole was taken off the project. He was reaching out to Ben for help with continuing the research.

"We're shut down at our university too," Ben interjected.

"It wasn't finished, Ben. I believe what they have taken is already being used in a devasting way. That is all I will say by phone. Please—I implore you to come immediately—my movements are quite restricted."

"I will have to discuss it with my wife. We keep no secrets from each other."

"That's fine, but please don't tell anyone else." When Ben did not respond right away, Dr. Cole spoke a short sentence foreign to most scientists, "Pray about it, Ben."

After relating the details of the conversation to Sara, she surmised, "He must be a Christian man. It sounds like he is trying to do the right thing here."

"We have a meeting with Pastor A.J. this afternoon. He wants to get to know us as a couple. They haven't shut down one day during all of this. No masks at church, or their pre-school. He heard you're a teacher, missing the kids."

"Maybe you're the one who told him,"...she nudged him.

"It will give us a chance to pray with him about meeting Dr. Cole, though."

"But we are not to say who we are meeting with, right?"

After the powerful message they had heard from Pastor A.J. the prior week, they were excited to speak further with this prophetic man at '*The Little White Church by the river*,' as it was called.

After a long prayer and some discussion on marriage, Ben finally asked, "How does one have their eyes opened to the truth, in the way God has revealed it you?"

"What is truth?" A.J. began. "Pontius Pilot, the Roman Magistrate scoffed these words to Jesus. Then he sentenced him to death. A lot of people will never know the truth, even when it is staring them right in the face. Nowadays everyone seems to be mocking the Bible and those who follow Jesus.

"Truth is not subjective. It is inerrant, like the Word of God. So, getting back to your question, *'How does one have eyes opened to this truth.'* Of course, it is first knowing scripture.

The Pastor slowly leaned back in his chair. A mist enveloped his eyes. "A few years back, we went through quite a rough patch. Sadly, our eldest daughter was killed in a roll-over auto accident during a storm. It took a toll on our marriage and even my faith for a while. Then one day I prayed a simple prayer."

"What was it?" Sara asked impatiently.

Pastor A.J. prefaced his answer carefully leaning forward in the worn leather chair, "It may change your life forever..."

"Please!" the couple said in unison, with a stare.

"The petition I made to our Lord God, our Father in Heaven, the Creator of all, in the name of Jesus Christ, were these five words: 'LORD GOD, SHOW ME EVERYTHING.'"

With the volume in A.J.'s booming voice, both Sara and Ben bent backwards in their chairs. "This prayer changed my life."

Pastor A.J. went on, "There is an old saying: *'Be careful what you ask for,'* and it pertains here. There is obedience and responsibility that comes with this truth. Sometimes people don't have *'Eyes to see, or ears to hear,'* but were called to *'Tell them anyway!'* God says."

"We're trying to seek the Lord daily together," Ben illuminated, "With all of our heart, soul and mind and *'Not be wise in our own eyes,'* as it says in Proverbs."

"It takes humility," A.J. counseled. "The Lord will reveal more if we remove ourselves from the worldly things and keep our eyes on heavenly things," A.J. gazed upwards.

"I'm sorry to hear about your daughter," Sara consoled; "we were friends with another pastor that lost his wife..."

Ben picked up the conversation: "He was a Preacher on fire for the Lord, whose wife died suddenly. He began taking pain killers to ease the burden and withdrew completely."

"When someone in Ministry isolates after tragedy, it is a sign the enemy is attacking them. Part of knowing deeper truth is having one's eyes opened to the workings of the spiritual realm. Our fight is not against flesh and blood, but against spiritual wickedness and the evil one." Ominously, a large dark bird began squawking outside.

"When you get home tonight maybe read the book of Ephesians together. Most ministers shy away from this important area of our calling. Ben mentioned you are studying Revelation together. The book of Daniel is a companion to what is unfolding. We are not only living in interesting times—but it is becoming apparent to me that we are living in the end times."

Pastor A.J. closed the Bible saying, "Let's close in prayer."

"We almost forgot!" Sara peered sideways at Ben, "Please pray for our travel tomorrow. We're heading to Raleigh."

Ben quickly explained the nature of the strange meeting scheduled with Dr. Cole. "I'm not really sure about this."

With a new tone, Pastor A.J. spoke in a soft hush, "Heavenly Father—creator of all things, bless Ben and Sara in their marriage, give them divine discernment, cover them with Your protective *Armor of God* and encamp Your angels about them as they go their way—In Jesus' Mighty name!"

"And show us everything!" Ben finished.

Winding down the Blueridge Parkway was a breathtaking drive anytime time of day or year. Now at dawn, peaks of the stunning mountain tops lit up in a bright orange as new growth lined the road. Ben sipped organic dark coffee from a ceramic covered cup.

Sara had reclined her car seat to rest. Dreamily, with eyelids closed she whispered, "How can anyone say all of this beauty happened by accident?"

Ben thought better than to question his wife this early, *Sara was often able to see things with eyes closed*, he smiled.

"Maybe they need to watch the Del Tackett series, *Is Genesis History*," Ben offered practically. "Many Darwinists are converting to the creation model now."

Sara deeply loved her husband, learning to live with the pragmatic comments, that often pruned romantic moments.

The natural splendor was quickly replaced with concrete and steel. New construction proliferated after veering onto Highway 29. Large neon signs were posted over the roadway every mile, or so. They carried a disturbing message:

"GO HOME – STAY HOME"

Sara noticed long convoys of National Guard Trucks heading in either direction, "There are a lot of Highway Patrol cars with flashers on too."

"We're one of the only cars on the road," Ben reinforced. He considered their white SUV may be less conspicuous,

Another concern intensified in Sara's voice: "Why are all these HUGE Cell Towers going up everywhere?"

"I've noticed them every mile, or two," Ben followed up. "Interesting time to be rolling them out with the plague to distract everyone."

"And everyone told to stay home," Sara raised her eyes.

Rapidly, a long line of white ambulances drove past them at high speed, followed by several long-black Hearses with the names of different funeral homes on the sides.

"This is like the *Twilight Zone!*" Sara cried out.

"Maybe they are conducting drills for this so-called pandemic," he replied wryly. "My Dad, the veteran, often said 'the Government doesn't always have your back.'"

"It's surprising no one has stopped us," Sara pondered.

"If there was really a National Emergency, this would have legal implications. So far, no laws have been passed. An illegal health directive by the CDC. They push mandates, but mandates are not law." Silently he prayed not to be incensed.

As they arrived in Raleigh, Sara commented, "I counted one hundred and twelve new giant cell towers, so far..."

Dr. Cole had instructed them to meet him in a location near his top-level government research facility. He had selected a popular chain restaurant for anonymity. *The ones along the highways must be open for all those involved with the new construction,* Ben considered.

Entering the lobby, the staff and patrons all wore face masks. A security guard was scanning people's foreheads to take their temperatures. Seeing a grey-haired man waving, Ben took Sara's hand and moved quickly past the guard forgoing any tests.

The older man sat alone in a large rounded booth; "Thank you for coming all this way," he said casually. "I'm Dr. Cole—we haven't much time."

Dispensing with the formalities, he reached inside a front breast pocket of his rumpled suitcoat and slid a large manilla envelope along the seat to Ben, saying "It's all in there."

Placing the package on his own lap, Ben felt it bulging towards the middle, "There are no samples, are there?"

"A report, with some electronics—a drive for backup." Nervously, Dr. Cole peered around the room, craning his neck. "Please wait to read this until you are safely home and study the materials thoughtfully—then pray about what to do regarding them." Arising from the table suddenly, he smiled for the first time, "May God go with you."

"Hold on," Sara sounded out. In a whisper, she quickly told Dr. Cole all they had witnessed on the drive to Raleigh.

"Besides all of the convoys, we counted over 100 large cell towers going up," Ben confirmed.

"5G," Dr. Cole said, turning to leave, "It is all a part of this Beast they are unleashing on the world."

As they began the journey back home, they each quietly processed the harried tenor of the clandestine meeting with Dr. Cole. They both sensed the package, now in their possession may come to pass on a grander scale.

Ben spoke first, "This infrastructure work must have been planned a while ago." Construction materials cluttered along both sides of the highway.

"Strange, I didn't spot that sign earlier," Sara pointed up while passing a new Military installation. The highway seemed almost deserted now. Long shadows fell across the roadway, as they contemplated all they had encountered.

"Drills must have ended for the day," Ben finally answered. Although the "GO HOME—STAY HOME," signs still flashed non-stop, becoming even more ominous as dusk fell.

Exhausted, after driving further, Ben suggested they stay the night and pulled into a high-rise hotel right off the road. Unloading the car, Sara eyed several National guard trucks parked out back.

"There are quite a few unmarked SUV's," Ben chuckled. "White government SUV's that look a lot like ours—no wonder they're leaving us alone."

In the guest area of the lobby, there were younger men in fatigues and older work crews milling around everywhere.

Entering the hotel room, Sara complained, "It smells like they are spraying toxic chemicals everywhere and none of these windows will open."

"I'm so tired, I could sleep in the car," Ben replied, "but not with these toxins..." Checking his cell phone he perked up, "Hey, it looks like there's a nice Bed and Breakfast in the nearby town with a room available!"

Shortly, they were nestling into a cozy Bed and Breakfast suite complete with an old cobblestone fireplace.

"This is more like it." Ben stretched out on the old King-size four poster bed.

Sara squeezed his toes in white socks. "Romantic too—and the windows open up to a garden with fresh air!"

In the morning, there was a note pinned on their door: "Help yourself to breakfast in the dining room."

On the long antique dining table lay several brown bags. Each had a croissant with cheese and a piece of fruit, "due to the pandemic," read another note.

"Well, that's one way to get out of making a delicious B&B Breakfast," Sara looked up disappointed.

"Same room cost though," Ben nodded, "let's get going."

At a gas station, Ben walked over to a young man wearing camouflage gear, "Thanks for your service," he began. Ben handed him a small white Bible the size of a matchbook. Pastor A.J. had encouraged them to "*grab a few handfuls*," from a table at church to share.

"There's one verse from every book in the Bible," Ben explained. My wife and I go on mission trips sometimes.

The soldier noticed Ben's Medical lanyard hanging from his neck. "Are you a doctor?"

Side stepping the question, Ben replied, "Good to see you're not wearing a mask. There was a report given by Dr. Fausti and the National Institute for Health, over a decade ago, saying they cause respiratory infections. They found the masks worn in the Spanish Flu pandemic, most likely caused pneumonia and millions of deaths."

"I'm breaking protocol," the soldier said, "sorry to tell you I'm sort of a rebel...I took it off for a smoke."

"Listen, our country was founded by rebels. I encourage you to remove the face covering whenever possible. Sometimes its better to follow God and your conscience."

"This is interesting," the guardsmen said, "My Mom is praying for me to quit smoking." Hopping up into the multi-colored camouflage truck, he ended, "Thanks for the Little Bible!"

"It may come in handy during a crisis," Ben waved. Driving out of the gas station he recalled the conversation with the soldier.

Sara responded, "Good job honey—I spoke with some younger ladies in the restroom. Sounds like none of them know anything."

After arriving home, Ben could not wait to open Dr. Cole's package. The Title of the report on top was foreboding:

U.S. ARMY ACTIVITY
IN THE U.S.
BIOLOGICAL WARFARE PROGRAMS
VOLUME 1 CLASSIFIED

"*The report on the top of stack is for background*," Dr. Cole had written on a large neon green post-it-note:

"Be extremely careful with who you share this information. Scientists who have faith in God, are more open to truth. Note: the term 'Conspiracy Theorist' was developed by the CIA in the 1960's as part of an MK Ultra plan to thwart those who knew they used Bio Weapons and Mind Control Drugs. What we face now, though, has eternal consequences for all humanity."

Ben flipped through the stack and noticed more neon notes; Dr. Cole's comments proliferated throughout. Retrieving the External Hard Drive, he wrapped it in plastic and taped it under his desk. Tomorrow would come early; Such information would best be digested when fresh.

On their home-office wall was a plaque that Sara made for him with her pre-school kids. It now drew his attention...

You shall know the Truth
And the Truth shall set you free
****

Chapter 4

'I planted you as a noble vine, wholly a right seed—How have you turned into a degenerative plant from an alien vine?' Jeremiah 2:21

Over the next several days Ben digested every aspect of the Cole Report several times. There were research studies, commentaries, graphs, charts and long-winded writings. Some of the information was redacted, or covered in black sharpie. Dr. Cole would often suggest what those deletions referred to in his notes. The Hard Drive was a treasure trove that would take longer to decipher.

Contents of the vast report were too sensitive to share aloud. Sara was led to read several parts of the documents privately. *Were they in breach of national security,* she wondered, *would they be monitored, or surveilled with this?*

Ben processed these matters through a filter of faith and curiosity first. Sure, they may already be listening in on phone conversations, computers, or a smart TV. It was his long-time habit to deactivate the router and cell phones, when working on sensitive material.

Each night they prayed together for wisdom and direction; putting on the *'Whole Armor of God,'* for protection, as they found in Ephesians 6. "Bind up the evil," Pastor A.J. had said.

Over the weekend, Sara and Ben were excited to attend the *Little White Church by the River.*

Moving in the Spirit, Pastor A.J. parted from a rote service, "We have a nice new faithful couple joining us today. I met with them this past week in my office. Ben and Sara can I ask you to tell us a little bit about yourselves?"

Ben and Sara took turns relating the details of their lives, giving testimony on how they came to know Jesus, as *born-again believers*. Sara told the story about how they met at the hospital finding love in the midst of their trials.

Ben finished by saying, "As a medical researcher, I just wanted to add that most of the churches in this area seem to be fear-based, from a clinical perspective."

"Seems spiritual too." Sara chimed in.

"Most wear masks or even meet in a church parking lot while staying in their cars during the service. Many people even wear a mask alone in their car." This drew a small laugh from the congregation. "Many churches have canceled services altogether. It is refreshing that you all seem to be so Holy Spirit filled. We love the scripture, *'for God does not give us a spirit of fear, but one of power, love and sound mind.'*"

"Amen!" Pastor A.J. answered from the pew.

After the service, Sara uncovered a cooler; "I made a picnic." Hiking to a nearby waterfall, she filled two paper plates with freshly made egg-salad sandwiches and home-made slaw. Sprinkles of mist gave cooling relief in the sunlight.

In between bites, Sara spoke in a serious tone. "This Cole report has captured your thoughts. You shared some of it with me, but it's a little over my head. If you had to sum it up in one concise statement, what would it be?"

Ben thought for a moment in repose, "This is not a fluke pandemic but one well-planned for many years. There is secret government involvement. It is leading to something that may compromise human DNA."

"Are they trying to contaminate the genome then?"

"That's a big part of it. Marshal revealed that his boss has been involved from the inception with researchers at MIT, working to encode biomatter. They met in New York right before the pandemic in the fall, under the cover name: *'Contagion Containment Plan.'*"

"Why in the world are they doing all this, Ben?"

"They strategized about implementing their diabolical 'plandemic' to control, track and deconstruct."

"That's a good name for it—'Plandemic.' So, it's about the virus?"

"From what I understand so far, they plan to use the DNA changing therapy, in so-called vaccinations to supposedly 'save people' from the virus they created. It may be for depopulation too."

Ben noticed waterfall tears forming in his wife's eyes.

Leaving her lunch, Sara climbed onto a nearby boulder closer to the powerful stream of water at the base of the falls.

By her response, Ben knew deep in his soul that all of this must be true. Wading into the water pooling all around them, Sara called out with forcefulness, "Well we did ask God to show us everything!" She extended her hand to help him onto the rock. "So—the final question is this: what do we do with this knowledge?"

That night before falling asleep, Ben whispered a prayer, "Please Lord, reveal to us the deeper secrets with everything happening, and how to expose them."

At daybreak, after more prayer, Ben received a word to read his Bible. Opening to the book of Deuteronomy, he read, ***"Chose life, that both thou and thy seed shall live."***

This is all about God's Holy seed, Ben thought. *About keeping it pure.*

Sara awoke later that morning, slowly descending the stairs of their mountain home. Gazing out the large glass windows something colorful was moving quickly outside. Laughing out loud, she realized it was her husband in his bright flannel shirt. Ben was tugging at some large pieces of lumber.

"What's going on out there?" Sara called from the deck in a gleeful tone.

"I remember you always wanted a real garden."

"Oh Ben!" Sara rushed with excitement in her nightie and embraced her husband. "Can I help?"

"Careful..." Ben replied. Sara inspected her slipper after side-stepping some steer manure. "You may want to put on some clothes first." Ben tried to contain his laugh.

He had been on a buying spree early that morning at the *Green Acres Gardens*. Besides the large bags of fertilizer, there were eight-foot-long boards, each a foot high and materials for a drip sprinkler system.

"I'm constructing four separate garden beds for you," he motioned hammering away. The neighbor woman gazed in their direction in bewilderment.

"Poor gal, she's wearing a mask," Sara hushed. "Outside!"

Ben smiled. "And you're still wearing a nighty."

After some organic oatmeal, fresh fruit and a change of clothing, the two worked all morning installing garden beds.

Finally, Sara interrupted their flow, "Let's go shopping!"

"Shopping again?" he leaned on a hoe, wiping a brow.

"For some seeds!" she gave a hearty laugh, "but let's buy only organic ones," she stated with determination.

At dinner they were exhausted from all their efforts. It was a wonderful feeling, however, to stare out the windows even in the pale light, at the four new garden beds. Seeds were planted and a drip irrigation system was already watering.

"This garden has been a welcome distraction from everything," Ben felt at peace for the first time in a long-while.

Handing him a dishtowel, Sara cajoled, "Then drying dishes will be a nice distraction for you too." Happily she reported, "There are four different kinds of tomatoes in one bed, Cucumbers, beets, radishes, kale, spinach, lettuce, broccolini, cauliflower and even peppermint."

"I don't have your expertise, but I know the peppermint can take over the garden, right?"

"It's in a separate bed," she explained. "Separate from the garlic and oregano you planted."

"Is that what it was?" Ben contorted his face. "Strong stuff— we could use some peppermint tea now before bed."

"Chamomile works well too—I bought a new box." Sara reached past Ben for the tea kettle.

Dark days of quarantine followed throughout the world. Panic driven by the media led to self-isolation, or imposed lockdowns. This led many to depression and loss of jobs. The division over quarantines and mask wearing intensified, dividing friends, families, liberals, conservatives and governments. Those who worked from home, often stared at TV's and their computer screens day and night. Drug addiction, alcoholism, divorce and even suicide proliferated.

One sociology professor Ben knew, casually mentioned,

"These *plugged-in people,* are becoming a part of the 'Meta.'"

Talk of a new type of vaccination surfaced that would save humanity. Ben was aware of each move ahead of time, with information from his nephew Marshal, the Cole Report and his own extensive research.

During his daily press conferences, the U.S. President reassured the country that all was well under control. At the morning briefings, Dr. Fausti of the NIH and Pharmaceutical industry patent holder, advised the President who promised, "We will be rolling out these shots at Warp Speed, with the Military!"

In further research, Dr. Cole's report served to confirm the pandemic events unfolding in every nation, were well planned. The United Nations agendas worked in concert with World Health and World Economic organizations. Wealthy elite met with heads of government in Davos Switzerland. Even the Catholic Pope aligned with the NWO power base.

For Ben and Sara, a homebound routine of prayer, exercise and intermittent fasting—with organic meals at noon—gave great fortitude and energy. The new garden was Sara's oasis.

Ben's respite was golfing weekly with Charlie and other friends. Most of the courses remained open without restrictions, for some reason, "Fresh air without masks," one golfer joked.

During their golf outings, all topics were discussed. Early on, Charlie had proclaimed, "I'm an evolutionist, so don't try any of that religion on me."

Teeing up his ball, Ben would try and slip in his faith, "The book of Revelation says the next big event is about to drop."

"Let's see if you can drop that ball into the hole," Charlie called out. "This par 3 is only 120 yards long..."

On their walk to the green, Charlie confided he was the one who circled back to their University Lab after the break-in, to put everything back in place.

"We were being set-up, Ben. I wanted to make sure it wasn't reported. They were either searching for our latest discovery, or wanted an excuse to keep us closed down."

"Dr. Pidgeon left a message yesterday," Ben responded. "He mentioned we may be opening up on a limited basis—we need to start independent lab testing, off the clock."

Just then, Ben's cell rang in his golf bag. It was Sara.

"Sorry to call. You may want to come home right away," she said nervously. Ben knew his level headed wife. This was not a frivolous call.

Arriving home in record time, Ben found his wife on the living room couch. She pointed at a neatly wrapped brown package, by the front door labeled: *'Bio-Hazard Materials, Time and Temperature Sensitive—Open with Caution.'*

Sara explained, "A driver left it by the front door. I was out back in the garden, but our neighbor spotted a black van leaving. She said it had an orange logo, or something on the side."

Ben eyed the small rectangular package suspiciously for a minute and then took it into the garage. Now for the first time since the pandemic began, Ben donned a protective mask. It contained a respiratory filter. He slipped on a thick windbreaker and found a pair of yellow rubber gloves.

Grabbing an exacto knife, the thin blade neatly sliced the package open, in his adept hands. Then, using a forceps and retractor, Ben extracted the contents. There were four Vials. Each was marked with different letters; P-M-A-J/J. The only words printed inside were: "Single Dose Vials."

Calling Charlie, they made arrangements to meet at the Lab in the morning, "We're going to claim access for a high-level event." His co-worker had found another discrepancy.

"It's a set-up! I just found an old can of *Lysol Disinfectant*. In the fine print it says: *'Kills the Coronavirus on contact.'*"

Back inside the home, Ben consulted the CDC-site typing: "What is a single-dose Vial?" The answer was what he suspected: *A single-dose 'VIAL' is a Vial of liquid medication intended for injection or infusion.*

After discussing the contents of the package over with Sara, they decided to consult the scriptures. The book of Revelation held answers for these current events, as foretold. Sara wrote with cursive neatly in her journal, as they studied the scripture together. It spoke about the many plagues to come upon the earth.

The 'VIALS' of Revelation, 16:1-2 KJV

16:1 "And I heard a great voice out of the temple saying to the seven angels, Go your ways, and pour out the VIALS of the wrath of God upon the earth."

16:2. The first poured out his VIAL upon the earth; and grievous sores (plagues) fell on the men who had the Mark of the Beast and worshiped his image...

"Why was the word changed from 'VIALS' to 'Bowls'?"

Read KJV and compare translations.

Mark of the Beast: "IN" the hand and "IN" the forehead. KJV

(not "On" the hand). Rev. 13:16-17

*18. **"And for by thy sorceries 'Pharmakeia'** (drugs, medicine) **were all nations deceived."** Rev. 18:23*

In the morning before driving to the Lab, Ben considered the task at hand. On the backseat of the SUV, sat the four vials in their subzero case, packed in a picnic cooler. Saying goodbye, Sara could not help but laugh after noticing he had strapped in the cooler with a seatbelt.

"Dr. Cole must have sent them to you," Sara whispered, while leaning into the car for a goodbye kiss.

Researching the contents of medical vials, however, was not part of his routine lab work. But now with the various vials to study, he and Charlie would switch gears.

As the large pines cast shadows along the road, Ben considered the path that led him this far. He was not truly a researcher in the medical field. When asked, Ben would simply respond, "My field is in genetic recognition."

Ben's doctoral dissertation at Duke University, had hypothesized that receptors on cells would open when a willing human subject was in agreement with receiving a medication, food, drink or information and closed when dissenting. He theorized that when a subject willingly accepted, or desired a medication administered, their cells and receptors were open to receiving it. Conversely, when the patient received a medication under duress against their will, cellular receptors closed off.

In their new research study, the control group was proving this hypothesis. A drug was less effective on an individual, overall, when they received the medication by force.

This was a companion hypothesis to the Epi-genetic breakthroughs Ben had helped discover at Duke. As director, of the new Lab, Ben gave his theory top priority.

For years, the Rockefeller medical school model, taught all that mattered in genetics was a person's family history. Ben was proving that 80% of the time, individual mindset and personal decisions were the primary factors for developing disease. Genetics and predisposition constituted for 20%, with individual decisions activating, or deactivating specific genes.

Studies revealed that a person with a pre-disposition for diabetes, for example, may activate the diabetes gene, by a poor diet and sedentary lifestyle. Conversely, diabetes was suppressed by eating a wholesome diet, rich in vegetables, healthy fats, with an active lifestyle.

A diet high in pork, sugar, carbs, drugs and alcohol usually 'switches on' the cancer genes, Ben published in one study;

The heavily controlled medical establishment and pharma industry oppose these genetic breakthroughs. Ben reported,

'The goal of Pharma is to create customers and not cures.'

Finally arriving at work, Charlie waited at the side entrance. "I disarmed the security system and cameras," he confessed. "The guard is busy playing video games..."

Sliding a keycard to the inner office, they moved inside.

"It still works," Charlie remarked quietly.

Walking quickly to the rear laboratory walls of glass, he waved to the motion detector. The inner door opened, revealing a vast array of research equipment.

Putting on white lab coats and gloves, Ben opened the cooler containing the four vials and carefully handed one to Charlie. Over the following hour, they worked quietly making notes while studying the vial materials. Charlie using a Confocal Microscope for cellular biology and tissue cultures, while Ben preferred the newer electron or fluorescence scopes, for magnification up to x1,000,000.

An hour later, the silence was broken, "You have to see this!" Ben recoiled, "It's a toxic mess!"

"Something appears to be moving," Charlie firmly gripped the eyepiece. "What are we looking at here?"

"It's the Moderna, I think," Ben illuminated, "Truly mind blowing—there's graphene oxide, hydra type of creatures, sharp metallic objects, nanotechnology and a lot more I have yet to identify—this mRNA permeates cells altering DNA."

"When I added the tissue cultures, to the 'P vial,' the mRNA spread spike proteins into the cells, and that black goo assembled like a magnet!" Charlie explained.

"Graphene oxide..." Ben shook his head.

Over the next several hours, they worked tirelessly without stopping. Absorbed in the work, at one point Charlie sneered, "It sort of takes away your appetite..."

As shadows deepened out the tall windows, they discussed their research, and for the first time, Charlie went on about his upbringing, "Mom was our protector." His father had been a strict disciplinarian, wary of the world.

"He marched our family right *out* of church one Sunday saying, *'All they want is your hard-earned money for another big church building!'* Dad joined a Masonic Lodge the next week."

Somewhat ironic, Ben surmised. *From one bad building program to another...*

"So that's why you're an atheist?" Ben asked.

"I would say 'agnostic.'"

"The difference between *'Ignorance and Apathy,'* is 'I don't know and I don't care,'" Ben countered. A wry smile formed at the corners of Charlie's mouth.

"Listen, I'm not going to push it on you, but scripture says, that *'Our bodies are Temples of God,'* and we are formed in His image." Ben paused, reaching for the J&J vial; "The Bible talks about 'Vials' and plagues being poured out upon the earth in the end times."

Neither of them said a word for what seemed like the longest time, contemplating the potential coming storm.

Finally, Charlie offered, "The Bates Foundation is already giving the injections to poor people in Africa and the homeless right here, in the good old U.S.A."

"There are none of the four-to-five-years of standardized trials," Ben added. "The pharma industry has complete immunity after making a deal with Congress years ago."

"Its late—we better get out of here and finish out these last two vials later on," Charlie motioned towards the cameras.

That night after prayer, Ben sent Charlie a message:

"Let me know if you want to discuss what the Bible says about the change of DNA and 'Mark of the Beast.' I believe it pertains to our discoveries today."

Chapter 5

"And the dragon was wroth with the woman, and went to make war with the remnant of her seed," Revelation 12:17.

A t Sunrise, Ben found his wife in the garden. Sara was miffed that her seeds were not sprouting. Those seeds that had broken the surface of the dirt appeared to be wilted. He bent down to study the ones that had sprouted, gathering a few samples.

Over a cup of coffee, Ben began sharing all they had discovered in the lab the night before. Before having a chance to finish all of the details, Sara jumped in, "Hold on Ben, there's a verse in Revelation, that I researched on my own last night. It seems to explain what's happening now."

Opening to Revelation 18:23, she read, *"And for by Sorcery all nations were deceived.'* Checking her margin notes, she went on; "When I studied the Strongs concordance in the original Greek text, I discovered that *Sorcery* means drugs, medicine, poisons, spells and even witchcraft!"

Ben read the scripture out loud again, saying, "It comes after the Chapters about the Mark of the Beast."

Seeing the concordance open to #5331, he read the section out loud, suddenly striking the passage with his fist; coffee spilling over the granite counters.

"Wow!" he exclaimed, "In the original Greek Septuagint, the word also translates *'Pharmakeia!'* " It came fast to him:

"This must be where the word 'Pharmaceutical' originates."

That night, Ben awoke after one of his powerful dreams, *"To much is given—much is expected."* Reaching for a notebook on the nightstand, he hastily scribbled the details:

In my dream, there was a tall thin man dressed in white, motioning with his arms. The palms of his hands were turned towards the ground, long arms circled frantically side-to side over a level field of scorched earth, appearing to stretch for miles in every direction. Then gazing upwards, slowly to the sky, two large white clouds melted together, turning dark. As the man in white raised his arms upwards, large raindrops began to fall—lightly at first. Then with a flash of lightning, skies burst open into a torrential downpour. Through the pouring rain, the man spoke these words:

"To much is given—much is expected..."

On their way to the *Little White Church,* in the morning, Sara responded to his dream. "Wow—that's a heavenly sounding message. A verse in the book of Joel says, *'Your old man will dream dreams and your young men will see visions.'*"

Tipping the rearview mirror his direction, Ben's fingertips brushed the thick hair, "Maybe I'm just getting older," he sighed. "There's a little salt and pepper now too."

Sara touched his cheek, "Dashing and handsome I'd say."

Turning onto a gravel side road, they parked at the old settlers church cemetery. It overlooked the rushing river.

In the cool air, Pastor A.J. nodded at the delipidated graves, "All these fine folks will have a nice view when Jesus comes back. The verse says, *'And the dead in Christ shall rise first.'*"

During the service, Pastor A.J. gave a blazing message:

"If you're looking for answers," he began, "then you have *'Ears to Hear'*...but if you are looking to argue about what the scripture says, then you *don't* have *'Ears to Hear.'*"

"Right now, there is a lot of confusion and contention between people about is happening in the world. But its coming from none other than that serpent—the devil. So far, he's succeeding—not only with a faithless world, but with Christians, by using fear over health. A true believer trusts in God.

"Listen, Satan is the author of confusion, accuser of the brethren and the author of lies. I want to begin by reading a scripture from the Book of Revelation Chapter 13:

*'And he causes all, both small and great, rich and poor, free and bond, to receive a mark in their right hand, or in their foreheads: And that no man might buy or sell, save he that had the mark, **or the name** of the beast, **or the number** of his name.'"*

"This takes wisdom," A.J. paused, wiping his brow with a white handkerchief. So, it says, 'there is a 'Mark' *'IN'* the hand or forehead. Isn't that different than '**On**' as all the other Bibles versions say? That's why we use the original King James here...it goes on to enlighten us that 'no man will be able to buy or sell, unless he takes *the 'Mark,'* '**Or**' has the name of the Beast, '**Or**' the number of his name.

Therefore, this 'Or' becomes quite important, doesn't it? It's not just '**On**' the hand or forehead, as most say, but *'In.'"*

A.J. carefully spoke the 'In' and 'Or' with great emphasis.

"In fact, they will not be able to *Buy or Sell*, unless they have *The Mark*, **Or** *The Name*, **Or** the *Number of his Name*. This calls for wisdom—*'let the person who has insight, calculate the number of the Beast, for it is the number of a man—that number is six hundred, three score and six.'"*

Pastor A.J. hesitated, letting the words sink in. "Thankfully, God seals all believers with *His Holy Mark* on the forehead. Even the prophet Ezekiel and Paul speak of the *Seal of God*; Whoever is *Born Again*, is sealed by the Holy Spirit."

"When the Beast is mortally wounded in one of its heads, the whole world will marvel at his recovery. It says *they worshipped the dragon that gave authority to the beast.'* So, who is the dragon?" he asked.

"It's the devil!" one younger girl cried out.

"That's my niece," A.J. laughed, "not fair," he said smiling her way, "because you already knew the answer..."

"It continues to say that the Beast will have authority for forty-two and a half months. That's three and one-half years, and will make war with the saints. Who are *the Saints*? They are those who are following Jesus Christ."

A.J. ended somberly. "We will have to be diligent, staying steadfast through persecution, enduring until the return of Christ. The Good News is we know who wins in the end—Why?—because we know the last page of this awesome book," he finished, holding up his old Bible.

After the church service, Sara chatted with some of the ladies and small children in the parking lot. Ben reached into the trunk and pulled out a package. Making his way past the old church cemetery, he spotted Pastor A.J. by the little river.

Handing him the package, Ben said, "I think its important you read this right away."

Later in the car, Sara asked, "What did you give the Pastor?"

"I gave him a redacted summary of the Cole report with my notes from what we discovered at the Lab the other night," he confided to Sara.

As they wound their way home up the steep mountain road, Ben became excited, "It came to me in the service what my dream might mean."

"What is it, Ben?"

"The man in my dream was spreading something around, when his arms were circling over the earth. He was sowing the ground."

"Spreading seeds!" Sara interjected.

"Exactly," Ben confirmed. "In other words, he was saying, *'When much is sown in obedience, more is watered by God.'* The *Soil* of God are those willing to share the truth, and the *Seed* is the Word of God, springing forth to guide the faithful.

The time is coming when those who love the Lord will need to warn those with *ears to hear*, like Pastor A.J. said today."

"Hard to believe all of these end-times prophesies from Revelation are happening in our lifetimes," Sara pondered. "Look!" she said suddenly, spotting a large eagle circling over the top of the tall pines. "Maybe it's a sign to keep going."

They drove in silence, Sara placing her hand on Bens' neck.

Ben knew his mission now would be to expose the truth. *The injections are part of a sinister and grander plan for all of humanity*, he contemplated; *designed to genetically modify and control every human being and their offspring. He would need to be discerning about getting out the Cole Report and their own discoveries after researching the Vials.*

"Better to be smart about it and fight another day," he said abruptly.

"What's that?" Sara murmured, having closed her eyes in meditation, for the past several miles.

"Nothing," Ben replied. "Just thinking about how to share the truth with everything coming."

At home, Ben printed off copies of the Cole Report and his research notes, while Sara made brunch. Their favorite dining spot on the raised deck had a picturesque view of the new garden. Ben gathered his thoughts, as he took a bite of the delicious veggie frittata Sara had whipped together.

"Dr. Cole possibly trusted other God minded researchers, to expose this madness," he clarified. "It's all unfolding now."

Over lunch, Ben went on to explain the Cole Report was actually a compilation of many coded government programs over the years, including bio-weapons. Drugs for manipulation were often used such as in *MK-Ultra*, mind control or *Project Chatter*, with using the truth medications.

There was a contemporary section referencing the recent mass shootings in America. Even before the lockdowns, it seemed that the airwaves were flooded with mass shootings at the hand of violent, enraged young gunman. Violence and shootings had escalated, affecting the nation's stability. The Cole Report indicated many mass killers were addicted to violent video games, but this information was to be suppressed.

Ben's own research found many of the youth involved in mass shootings were sadly from single parent homes and the young men were often on pharmaceutical drugs for 'ADD,' 'schizophrenia,' or 'depression'. *Another coverup to what end? Was this another program designed for gun control?*

The media debate raged daily over gun control and many stalwart patriots worried the 2nd Amendment was being usurped, by a federal government seeking to take the guns from citizens, for control, as happened in Nazi Germany.

At dusk, Ben had another secure video call with his nephew, who shared, "Hey—I took your advice and read the entire book of Revelation. People think it's a Vision by His disciple John, but it says: *'The Revelation of Jesus Christ.'*"

"That's right," Ben agreed. "So what did you discover?"

"A little hard to figure out. Some crazy stuff in there. But it does talk about the *Mark of the Beast* a few times."

Ben explained the message they had heard that morning about the *"In"* the hand or forehead not *"On,"* and about the '*Name or Number of his Name, needed to Buy and Sell.*

"Wow!" Marshal perked up, "didn't realize they talk about all those things at church."

"This one does…" Ben started to mention the Cole report, but caught himself from revealing too much, even over the encrypted line his nephew devised.

"There's something I need to share with you, but better not say much here—it deals with your Mr. Bates."

"He's not 'mine' Uncle Ben," Marshal said defensively. "I can't wait to quit my job—but maybe I can find out more while I'm still here. Bates wants the entire world on lockdown. This is called; **Problem – Reaction – Solution**. They create the problem, *the Plandemic* with a run-away virus. Then they use the media and governments to get everyone to *React with Fear*."

"And the Solution, is the mRNA injection for every man, woman and child on earth." Ben replied with concern.

"With the coding in it," his nephew sighed. "With a patent ending in 060606, like the number in Revelation. Hoping I'm not going to Hell for being a part of it," Marshal cast his eyes downward.

"That's where something called *Repentance*, comes in," Ben offered, "I'll send you something on *forgiveness* and our Lab Research, after we tested a few vial samples from the shots."

"How did you get a hold of those?" Marshal seemed rattled.

Realizing he may have revealed too much, Ben kept cool saying, "Oh, the Labs have access to a myriad of things…" he held a finger up to his lips over the video call.

Picking up on the clue, Marshal said, "hold on a minute." Writing quickly on a pad, he held it up to the screen. There were several names: *WEF/Davos, Klaus Schnob, the WHO, Tedros, DARPA, G7: Windsor, Trudeau, Schultz, Macron, Blair. Bates/Epstein.*

The following morning, Ben drove to meet several colleagues and other doctors to share parts of the Cole Report and his own independent research.

"They have totally discounted natural immunity," one researcher mentioned.

There was a visceral reaction from another older doctor, so Ben retrieved the report right from his hands.

Interesting, Ben considered, *the ones I know who are faithful remnants, are more open to discovering the truth.*

At lunch, Ben's cell rang, "Oh no Ben!" his wife sounded agitated, "Our old Springs Church called. Its going way beyond the parking lot services. Now they're bussing people to get vaccinated at the pharmacy!"

"That's evil," Ben bemoaned, maybe you can warn them by sharing one of the videos we received from Dr. Madej, or Zelenko.

That night at home, Sara lamented further, "I posted the warning videos on the church website, but it started a huge firestorm. Even the pastor weighed in asking for us to take them down..."

"We're going up against a Goliath with the pharmaceutical industry," he responded. "They're the largest industry in the world now."

"Maybe, but I didn't expect the Churches to become their pushers!" Sara's nose crinkled when she became agitated. "And we're fighting fear. People trust in man and medicine over God and Jesus, for protection, provision and healing."

"Goodness Sara!" he responded. "Sums it all up."

Ben gave his wife a reassuring good-night peck on the cheek. Reaching for his nightstand notebook he wrote: *'With fear they trust in man and medicine over the Lord.' Isn't there a verse that says 'those who trust in man will be cursed and those who trust in God will be blessed?'*

Then he added a note to himself: *'Remember to take video series to work for Charlie tomorrow: 'Is Genesis History?'*

Chapter 6

"That in His mercy, God will preserve a remnant," Hosea 4:6

That following year, Ben and Sara did everything in their power to warn about the hazardous 'vaccinations' being given throughout the world. Pastor A.J. had preached not to be offended when friends or family members are in opposition, or become agitated, "It's a Biblical principle when exposing the truth," he reminded.

Through lectures, articles and shared research, Ben reported his findings about the evil contents in the shots.

Sara contacted everyone she had ever known and pleaded with them, "Please—say no to these experimental DNA changing injections. Let's stay made in the image of God."

In the fall, a new U.S. President was elected, amid a controversial race charged with election fraud. The liberal administration was even more pro-vaccination. They pushed mandates for government workers, the military, health care workers, education and first responders. States became even more polarized with the South resisting the mandated tests, vaccinations, while protesting any new Passport ID Cards.

Rallies began forming with thousands of mandate resisters. Marches spread from Washington D.C. across America, to Europe and Australia, opposing what was labeled as *"The Medical Tyranny."* Many lost not only relationships with friends and family members over these convictions—many lost their livelihoods, homes and marriages.

On the other side, a group called "'Antifa,' spread violence and mayhem in the cities. "We get paid by George Sorgross," one leader revealed. It was reported that Sorgross, an elite liberal billionaire, was behind much of the dissention nationwide.

Mandates called for unprecedented testing with a PCR swab pressed and twisted far into the naval cavity.

"Imagine a virus so deadly, that one has to take a test to discover if you even have it!" Charlie would say at work.

"The inventor of the PCR test, K.T. Mullis, has come out against its use for this," Ben mentioned one day at the lab.

"He just died, Ben—Mullis was a Noble prize winner. Kept saying it wasn't designed to detect infectious diseases."

"Maybe that got him killed."

The media fueled division nationwide, over the contested national elections. Protests and debates over quarantines, health mandates and the injections, proliferated. Liberals aligned with lockdowns and the media world narrative. Conservatives seemed to align with faith, at first more reluctant to take the shots.

Late in summer, distressing family news came that Sara's twenty-year-old niece, a junior at USC, was in a California hospital. There had been an immediate reaction to the Moderna; anaphylactic shock. The family was barred from having any direct contact with her. They feared she may even be on a ventilator.

By the time Ben and Sara called to suggest forming a rescue party, her brother answered in tears, "She's dead, Sis! The hospital said Callie died alone in the middle of the night—I was just calling you," he sobbed.

With trepidation they attended the funeral, across the country. Airports were a ghost town. With churches and mortuaries closed for funeral services, the event was held in a backyard with a handful of people. A sad affair. Sara read scriptures from Psalms: *"Even though I walk through the valley of the shadow of death, I will fear no evil..."*

THE FINAL SEED

Ben was heartsick over the change to the State, since he had attended College in Northern California years earlier. "It feels like we are in Sodom and Gomorrah here."

"Or even worse," Sara added.

The twenty-four years had flown by, since Ben had excelled as an undergrad at Simpson. One of his early mentors, Dr. Bryan Booker, a Biologist, was one of the first to expose the evils of modern vaccinations. A whistleblower at the Centers for Disease Control, Dr. Will Thompson confessed on recorded calls with Dr. Booker, Ben's professor. The CDC had destroyed and omitted crucial data on the safety of the shots.

The professor's own son was a victim of the *MMR* shot. A dire cocktail for mumps, measles and rubella. Many children had developed debilitating autism or died from the inoculations. In response, Dr. Booker, was featured in a documentary film called *Vaxxed* with director Del Bigtree. It struck Ben to the core, after helping on the project, as an undergrad; he would never again view medicine or vaccines in the same way.

Now back in California, evil State Legislators, along with Tech and Hollywood, had tainted the soil. Taxpayers were obligated to pay for sex-change operations; even for children without parental consent. A same sex agenda was pushed in schools, and counselors were forbidden to help those wanting to leave the lifestyle. Abortion on demand proliferated throughout campuses statewide. Euthanasia was becoming legalized for all ages. Sara mentioned seeing a TV commercial glorifying the assisted suicide process, showing a young woman in a wheel chair at the beach, with harp music, friends and family cheering her on...to death.

If that wasn't evil enough, a new law passed the State Legislature. Assembly Bill 2223 exonerating parents, doctors and medical staff for allowing a baby to die up to 28 days after birth. The legalized killing of babies born alive!

After hearing the news that evening Sara burst into tears, "How dare them! All those poor innocent children. The wicked ones doing this would be better to have a millstone tied around their neck and drowned in the ocean! "

Ben switched-off the TV in their hotel room, holding her tight and saying, "Vengeance is mine, sayeth the Lord."

Heading back home from LAX, Ben heard someone say the puffed-up phrase, *As goes California, so goes the Nation...*"

"I felt like making a sign and standing on a street corner,"

"What would it say?" Sara wondered.

"Simple—it would say: '*Repent California!*' on one side and '*Only Jesus Saves,*' on the other..."

Back home, they took a brisk country walk after dinner.

Sara considered, "If someone is required to take an injection to keep their job, then it already becomes like '*buying and selling.*'"

"Like it says in Revelation," Ben responded. "They need a job, for the money just to buy and sell. A lot of preachers are saying this is a *'Precursor'* to the *Mark of the Beast*, but I can't find that word or concept anywhere in the Bible."

"Well, it does say in Romans, 'God will have mercy on whom he will have mercy,'" Sara raised her eyes, "I hope so."

"But why would anyone risk their eternal salvation on something like this?"

Sara waved to their next-door neighbor, Lady Lee, who was watering her lawn, while wearing a paper-thin blue mask.

"She never waves back," Ben raised a hand, "the lawn's looking great, Lee!"

"I've invited her for tea and to our ladies' group at church a few times, but she always comes up with an excuse."

That Monday, Sara was elated to receive a message from her principal at the school. "The academy is opening next week!" She beamed at the prospect of seeing her preschoolers.

Sara's elation was short-lived, however, after a school nurse called. "They are mandating the shots, Ben! I can't believe this new nurse set an appointment for me. They give them right on campus!"

After prayer with her ladies' group, Sara knew God's plan.

Within a week, she had quit her job and opened her own pre-school with three other mothers and a handful of kids. The fellowship hall where they taught, was given gratis and operated under a 'God-given exemption,' she told others.

After niece Callie's death, Sara's brother, a teacher himself, found a new calling, exposing the shots and evil hospital protocols. Appearing on several conservative news segments, Tomas rallied against mandated Remdesivir and other deadly drugs, for Covid patients. He stated ventilators were death traps.

"Just track the money," he reported. "Hospitals are paid thousands for each Covid diagnosis and far more for each Covid death. Our daughter Callie is one of untold thousands, young and old who are dead or dying, from the shots and protocols. *NOT* a fake Covid Virus!"

"These payments to the hospitals are incentive for murder," Tucker Carlson responded on one program.

While a fear-based country cowered indoors, there was one lone man traveling to ten major cities. He dressed in sackcloth and ashes proclaiming God was judging the United States, "Repent, for your evil deeds!"

"Hey—this guy's like my sign idea for California," Ben burst out one night. "Let's watch this man's daily feed."

Over the following ten days, Ben and Sara did a sundown fast and watched the man wearing sackcloth nightly.

"*Repent San Francisco*, for your sexual sin! *Repent Los Angeles and Hollywood,* for your filthy content! *Repent Houston and Planned Parenthood,* for murdering babies!

Repent New Orleans, For your drunken ways! *Repent New York—Babylon*—for your love of money and whoring ways!"

One by one to all 10 cities, this brave young man would proclaim the Gospel message of Jesus and salvation while warning that "the Kingdom of Heaven is at hand."

Finally, after arriving in Washington D.C., during the inauguration, the man wearing sackcloth and ashes stood preaching in the middle of a deserted street. Tall electric fences had been erected all around the Capitol.

After just a few minutes of sharing his testimony, the D.C. police and National Guard stationed around him, cordoned off the area. *"Repent United States! Repent!!!"*

"We have you surrounded!" one short-haired woman in a blue uniform called out through a megaphone. "Place your hands over your head now and keep them there, or we will open fire!"

"There are marksmen with rifles on you," said another cop.

Complying, the man stood motionless with arms raised in a 'V' position. Then a man filming from a distance, encouraged him, "Keep on preaching, Brother! A dying world is watching—there's never been a better time to share the Gospel."

For the next hour, the man in sackcloth, spoke with great authority filled with the Holy Spirit. A message poured forth of grace and forgiveness by the atoning blood of Jesus Christ.

"He died on the cross for all who believe on Him. He's coming back in the clouds of glory to return for his faithful remnant!"

At one point, the man in sackcloth whispered to his friend filming, "Man, are my arms tired..." They had lowered from the 'V' now. Outstretched side-to-side, as on the cross.

The faithful cameraman replied, "Think about how Jesus must have felt." The videographer then turned the camera lens on the police, explaining the man in sackcloth was not a terrorist with a bomb, but a nation-wide preacher. "Jonah in the Bible dressed in sackcloth and ashes," he reminded.

Straight away, several black presidential limousines sped past them through the intersection. Shortly thereafter, loud static sounded from around the captain, who reached up to touch his earpiece. After a pat down, the man in sackcloth was released.

After watching the live feed, Sara and Ben sat stunned. "What the devil meant for evil—God used for good," Ben whistled quietly.

The following morning at the men's Heavenly Grounds Bible study, Ben shared the story about the man in sackcloth and ashes. He was surprised that none of the men knew about it. The media had buried the story.

"All of the pastors at the Mega Churches get coverage for promoting the shots," Pastor A.J. weighed in.

"The past President, pushing the injections, convened a committee headed by 'Pastor' Paula White. It included all the big names; Falwell, Jeffress, Graham, Laurie, Copeland..."

"Franklin Graham said Jesus, and his dad would have taken this vaccine," a dark-haired man replied tenuously.

"Jesus *is* our vaccine!" an elderly man shot back.

"Churches have become big business," A.J. bemoaned.

"The government bribes the churches with their *'Paycheck Protection Act,'* I assure you; we will refuse to take a dime."

"Some of the Churches like Lakewood, have already taken millions of dollars from the feds," one man added.

"It's a Covid deception—they become obligated to help with the vaccinations," Ben pointed out.

Over the next hour, the twelve men delved into a study of Daniel, who was not afraid to speak the truth to King Nebuchadnezzar in Babylon. Pastor A.J.'s son, James, prayed to close the meeting: "Help us to prepare, Lord, and trust that *You* will be with us, when we are called to *'Speak before Kings.'*"

That evening, Ben lamented to Sara after ending a call with an old friend, "I can't believe Dave and Jill are getting a divorce. They were always so rock solid with their faith together—four children too."

"Oh no! Was it over the shots?" Sara asked with intuition.

"Yeah, she got the Pfizer a few months ago and didn't tell him; took their oldest daughter in for a shot behind his back."

"How sad," a tear formed in the corner of Sara's eye. "It may ruin her reproduction."

"Studies from Scandinavia and Europe are showing the female reproductive organs can become damaged," he confirmed. "They lied about doing the trials and research here in the States," he spoke somberly. "They gave the injections right at their Mega Church..." Ben had fumbled for the right words to use, on the call with his old friend about the divorce.

Dave had mentioned living in upstate New York, where his wife had refused to let him back into the home without the dreaded shots. "I'm living above the garage, in a cold drafty loft," he reported, "Child Protective Services and the Health Service Agencies are completely on her side."

Finally, an encouraging verse came to Ben: "Remember *'He who endures to the end shall be saved.'* Hang tight buddy—especially for your children."

At bedtime, a voice message came in from Pastor A.J. *"I'm finally reading your reports. Staggering information; hoping to discuss it before my next sermon. I'm giving a message on the Nephilim in Genesis Chapter 6. Please read. The fallen angels, demons, 'came into the daughters of men,' resulting in a race of Giants upon the earth. It would have changed their DNA, right?"*

Later in the week, Ben and Sara attended a town meeting.

There was division over mandating the shots for the public workers. Council members were vocally at odds.

The Mayor interjected, "I was sicker than a dog after one AstraZeneca shot—I vote *'NO'* on any mandates!"

Without revealing too many details, Ben spoke briefly on the poisonous contents found in the vials. "We need to consider how these will alter DNA genetically," he cautioned.

One Pathologist denounced: "They give the tests and shots to people who then get a Covid flu, and then seek medical solutions. The hospitals receive buckets of money to diagnose patients with Covid. They are forced to administer lethal drugs, like 'Remdesivir', forced to place people on ventilators. The hospitals receive even more money for a Covid death. All the while, early treatment plans that work, such as Ivermectin, or natural HCQ, Hydroxychloroquine, are prohibited."

"You people are all so selfish!" a middle-age lady called out, "we will never reach the herd immunity unless we all *'take one for the team!'*"

"People are not cows," the Mayor replied, to a hearty laugh.

A slight Cardiologist stood up saying, "We're starting to see Mitochondrial signs with heart inflammation." In three to five years, the only solution is a heart transplant..."

A Respiratory Therapist Sara knew, said she was fired from the Hospital after refusing to take the shots; Karin also refused to use the ventilators or Remdesivir, "They shut down the organs!" she announced. "Some of us have hired lawyers."

Another nurse spoke out abruptly: "I call Remdesivir: *'Run—Death is Near!'*"

Walking to the car after, Sara was surprisingly upbeat, "Glad we live in Mountain Rest, where they pray before the meetings and vote against any mandates..."

"For now," Ben remarked. "We do have freedom of speech."

The drive home seemed darker through the dense forest.

Sara recalled one sobering conversation, "One Christian lady I knew there, mentioned attending a *Healing Hearts* conference. She sat between two women, who just received their first shots. They were all good friends and hung out together. A day after the two-day event, she started her menstrual period. Said she had never taken any jabs and was convinced it was from sitting between her two recently vaxxed friends. Get this—she's seventy years old!"

"It's called *Shedding*," Ben muttered.

"Shedding can happen when the live virus, or spike proteins from a vaccination, move through the body, and are 'shed', or released, through saliva, nasal discharge, feces, coughing or even breathing." Ben made a mental note while driving; *Research more about Vax Shedding tomorrow at the Lab. Will they transmit through electromagnetic frequencies, or sexual contact?*

Finally, their *day of rest* came. Ben dragged himself out of bed half-awake, searching for the coffee grinder. *Nothing better than a peaceful Saturday with a waterfall hike later. A favorite scripture in Exodus read: "My Sabbaths you shall keep: It is a sign between me and you throughout generations."*

The respite was fast broken, hearing his wife on a call from the deck, "That's terrible dad!"

A minute later, spotting him in the kitchen, Sara motioned with wild arm waving to join her.

The phone held tightly at her side, she whispered to Ben, "My father succumbed to the first Pfizer injection." With a dejected look, she handed him the phone.

"Well, please—don't take any more dad," Ben interceded.

"All of our lab research has shown this is anti-health. Technically, it's not gene therapy either. As you stated yourself last year, it *doesn't* fit the medical definition of a vaccination. And you were the one that educated me saying, 'A virus mutates too quickly for any vaccination to ever be effective.'"

At lunch, Sara bemoaned further, "Here my dad's an M.D., a well-respected Endocrinologist for over forty years, a *Rhodes Scholar*, and he takes the poison! At his new fancy retirement community, they told him to take it or move."

"Don't forget he sings in the church choir."

"I suggested a Christian center, but he paid them a ton of money for a life-care contract. On top of it they are mandating a weekly PCR test up the nose," she said, fired up.

"I read in a new report it may break the blood-brain barrier."

In the morning, Ben received a message from Dr. Pidgeon at work. "The University is reopening next week," he stated.

"Any research you have worked on during the lockdowns must be submitted for my department review."

"Didn't they mandate the shots?" she asked with concern.

"It's incredible," the corners of his mouth curled upward. "They approved my exemption letter, based on faith."

"That's great then, I guess—it's been a nice long time together with you..."

"My favorite lockdown," he smiled.

Sara was torn while preparing for bed that night. Her mind began racing. *In a way, these months alone together were so special. Ben liked his morning runs on the well-groomed Crystal Lake trail. The nearby abandoned State Park had been their playground. He could circumnavigate the lake in forty minutes. 'Its a Biblical time,' he said. Sara occasionally swam in the bright waters of the cool lake during his runs. Across and back before he makes it around. In the early evenings, after gardening, she joined him golfing on a few holes, or a short waterfall hike.*

Ben often commented that her healthy Keto cookin' kept him in shape; *unlike those paunches on most men his age,* she chuckled to herself. Most likely, giving up the drinking a decade earlier, helped to keep the years off both of them. Nestling under the covers, Sara's thoughts cascaded into the past again. Over a decade long gone, yet still engrained. It was her miscarriage that often resurfaced at these times.

Four and a half months along. Ben had found her on the floor, calling for help. While her life-blood drained, all was handled right there at home; with the help of a neighbor. A Naturopath. Instead of driving a wedge into their marriage, her recovery served to draw them even closer together and closer to God. Her husband had been so attentive and nurturing. An ensuing year-long struggle with sorrow had led to a bad mood lifting pharmaceutical. It only served to make matters worse.

On one occasion, when someone reported their dog had died, the mood-altering drug spoke for her, "Well then you don't have to worry about Rex anymore." She might even laugh at what had come out of her own mouth. *At other times, such as a dinner party, she might become depressed and wish to dispense with the pleasantries, forcing Ben to drive her home.* But by their enduring prayers and reading powerful scripture aloud together, a transforming moment finally came.

In their weakness, God was strong. One night, again on the floor together in a sober and repentant moment, God released them from these demonic strongholds. The Lord had delivered her from the addictive drug and both of them from the spirits of alcohol, all in that same night.

Now as Ben slid under the sheet next to her, she held him tightly. "God is our great physician," she whispered. "But you make a good one too..."

Ben said a prayer and leaned over for a good night kiss. *Sometimes its better not to ask,* he pondered. *Sometime its better to trust that God has got this one...* "Sweet dreams, my love—sweet dreams..."

Chapter 7

"That in blessing, I will bless thee and thy seed and in multiplying, I will multiply thy seed as the stars of the heaven," Genesis 22:17

Early in the morning, as Ben slept, Sara came rushing into their bedroom, "None of the garden seeds seem to be sprouting—they're all wilted." She tugged at the covers to stir Ben awake. "There is a man in Greenville, who can help. Wakeup sweetie, I'll buy you breakfast at the Cracker Barrel."

Sara had heard about Mr. Green, *The Heavenly Gardener*, from a friend. It made no difference driving the two hours from the mountains to his nursery, outside of Greenville.

Mr. Green stood alone in the center of a lush Garden. His organic nursery rivaled the best in the country. "Grampa Green," as he was known, said, I've been potting and growing beautiful gardens for over 35 years—given a plant or two...

"An appropriate city name of 'Greenville' too," Ben laughed. "Wonder why no one else is here?"

"For the longest time I've been studying the workings of an organic garden, Mr. Green, but only a few of these seeds are sprouting." Sara frowned, handing him several empty seed packets.

The older black man was shorter with a wiry frame, although his thick forearms told a different story. "It's a wonder that any of your plants spread at all with these packets. They're genetically modified."

"They're GMO?" Sara recoiled. "They told me all of these were natural."

"Naturally," Grampa Green laughed. "They say everything is natural now. Cuz, you got to read the labels now. It's all junk, like the processed foods. You can't pronounce it—don't buy it..."

Ben been chimed in, "I recently read a report that the chemically processed foods have led to millions of deaths."

"Sounds like you all know what's going on then," Grampa replied.

Later at the register, while buying the new organic seeds and potted plants, Sara calmly asked: "You're a believer in Jesus, aren't you Mr. Green?"

"Don't leave home without Him," came the response, as he started singing: *'Well they tell me of a home far beyond the sky, they tell me of a home faraway. Where the Tree of Life in eternal bloom, spreads it fragrance on the unclouded day.'*

Sara and Ben joined in on the last refrain: "Where the tree of life in eternal bloom—on the unclouded day."

"One more thing, Mr. Green," her voice lowered, "You do know about these genetically modified shots, don't you?" It was hard for her to ask the question. Several other people had flared up to condemn her after asking. *This time it came more easily*, she thought.

"FOOLHEARTY! Foolhardy!" he replied, "the Serpent's poison, as far as I'm concerned." He looked around at the impressive garden, the fragrance of lavender filled the air. "Maybe that's why there's only a couple of people like you out on a beautiful weekend like this. Not ashamed to tell people about staying made in God's image..."

"Or your incredible God-given seeds," Sara smiled. "Is it okay if we hug you goodbye Grampa Green?"

"Well let's not make it a permanent goodbye," he reached out to embrace them both. "I'm sure we'll see each other in heaven one day, if not before." With a broad grin, Gramps handed her hand-written planting instructions.

"On the unclouded day then, if not before," Ben waved, pushing a large cart and singing until getting into the car.

The following morning, the *Little White Church* rocked again, with Pastor A.J.'s message: "One reason the country is in such a mess is because they removed God from the schoolhouse, the courthouse and almost every house in the land!" he bellowed, "so the Lord must have said to himself, 'Then if you don't want me—I will forsake you...'"

At that moment, Sara nudged her husband in the pew, "Look, who's here," she whispered. Ben surveilled the room;

Charlie! He smiled to himself. *He must have watched, 'Is Genesis History' this weekend.*

Charlie remained standing by the front church door, even though Ben motioned him over.

"Many of you already know where I stand on these mandates, protocols and shots." A.J. continued, "So today my message concerns what the Bible reveals about this from the start. When God created Adam and Eve, their DNA was perfect. But after the sin of Satan came into the world the DNA was corrupted. His sin was Pride and he wanted to be God. With changing the DNA, he wants to play God.

"When Death entered in, the genetic information became corrupted. What are the genetics of the mark of the beast? How does Satan plan to cause mankind to take his DNA?

"The whole Saga begins in Genesis 3:15., in the scripture, God tells Satan, *'I will cause enmity between you and the woman, your seed and her seed, he shall bruise your head and he shall bruise your heel.'* If her seed is representing Jesus Christ, then the devil's seed is referring to the Antichrist; we have to look at the genetics of that. The incarnation. Corrupting the image. The Seed.

"When the Bible talks about seed what is it talking about? It's not just talking about something we put in the ground and a daisy pops up. Think of a watermelon seed, what is that? We can feel it, there's a husk, inside there's a kernel, inside the Chromosomes are the Genes, and the DNA."

A.J. picked up his notes and kept on, "There's a double helix, nucleic acid, still what is all that? It's the hardware, it's the software. DNA is the source code of humanity. It's the essence of seed that scripture so often refers to. The term seed in modern terms is called a gamete, which in a male is the sperm and the female is the ovum. Thus, when Mary conceived, it meant that her ovum provided 23 chromosomes and the Holy Spirit provided the seed from God.

'The sons of God were fallen angels, the same that Jude and Peter spoke about, that are kept in Chains of Darkness reserved for judgment. They came to the daughters of Adam and from their union were born the Nephilim, creating human demonic genetic material. The Fallen Angels and the demons are one and the same.

"The Nephilim, or the Fallen ones, we're the Giants known as *The Mighty Men of the Earth*. God later told Joshua and then David to cleanse these Nephilim out of the promised land. Remember Goliath?

"God says to reproduce according to your kind and the demons, the Fallen Angels when they came into the daughters of men, broke this command. When Satan sees that he will be crushed by the seed of Eve—so in turn the devil does all he can to destroy the seed of man."

A.J. paused briefly downing a big glass of water. "Are you following all this? Could the Devil be trying again to corrupt mankind's DNA, once again?

"All of the ancient Greek and even Jewish traditions believe that the Nephilim were hybrids only half human. The other half demonic. King Og, of Bashan in the Bible was about 15 feet tall, Canaan was the land that *'devoured its inhabitants.'* Cannibalistic. The inhabitants were the Nephilim and God called for the extermination of the seven nations when the children of Israel came into the land.

"The genetic mingling could not be tolerated just as it could not be tolerated back in the days of Noah, when God opened all the floodgates.

"So, Satan tried to destroy all of the humankind and tried to destroy Jesus when he came on the Earth. Thank God he failed in all these attempts. And now we're facing another one of these times when the evil one is rearing his ugly head to change the DNA of man—most people are 'partying on' like in the days of Noah.

"So—what's the answer then? First of all, I would think twice about taking this..." A.J. formed his index finger like a needle poking into his shoulder, "Remember that motto: *'Just say no to drugs!?'*

Then holding up the large Bible, he read:

'When all my people who are called by my name, humble themselves and pray and seek my face. When all my people turn from their wicked ways, then I will hear from heaven, I will forgive their sin and I will heal their land,' sayeth the Lord. 2nd Chronicles 7:14.

"Isn't God saying we need to *repent* of all our evil ways, in this passage?" Stroking his beard, the Pastor seemed to look across the room straight at Charlie. "So, who will take our sin on when we ask?"

"Jesus!" replied a petite older lady wearing a pink hat.

A.J. flashed a big smile extending his arms sideways. "Its called the 'Good News,' the *Gospel Message*. Jesus died on the cross for our sins, He rose on the third day from the tomb, ascended into Heaven and sits on the right hand of God the Father..." Dramatically, A,J. gazed upwards and finished, "Jesus of Nazareth, King of all Kings and Lord of *ALL* Lords is coming back again, for all those who believe on Him!"

"Amen Pastor!" Smiled the lady in the pink hat.

After the service, A.J. thanked Ben for his reports. "Helped me with the message today." Then nodding to Charlie who was heading out-the-door, he suggested, "Hope your friend didn't leave right away on my account—the Word often cuts like a sword..."

That night, Ben had big news, "They're organizing a week-long conference with all of the medical professionals opposed to the narrative and protocols. We've been asked to attend with all of our expenses paid." The Medical Freedom Conference would meet in Cozumel, a quaint Island off the Caribbean coast of the Yucatan Peninsula. It was comprised of those *Freedom Doctors and Scientists* aligned for medical truth.

"One of those dry medical conferences?" Sara frowned.

"Oh, I forgot to mention, its being held on an Island in the Yucatan."

"Why the Yucatan?" she asked.

"We fly through Cancun, Mexico. It's the only place on earth left open without any Covid restrictions—no masks, no tests, no shots."

It was not difficult for Ben to enlist his wife to attend, after further explaining their afternoons would be free. "How about some snorkeling, exploring Mayan ruins, street fairs, or relaxing poolside?" he coerced.

"The warm turquoise waters of the Caribbean will be perfect after this cold spell were having," she said dreamily.

At dawn, Sara flew down the stairway to check on her garden beds. It had been several weeks, since planting the organic seeds, hand-selected by 'Grampa Green.' To her delight, most all of the varieties of vegetables were sprouting! Small straight stems and bright little green leaves proliferated throughout the soil.

THE FINAL SEED

While tending to the garden and plucking out a few tares, she considered what to pack for the coming trip to Cozumel. *It would be such a relief from the quarantines and the fear she sensed in others eyes, 'With the masks all smiles disappeared overnight...' Ben would be attending most sessions with the other medical professionals, providing time during the day for her to relax, read, swim and pray. Their afternoons open to explore. Ben had promised, 'a special time for our marriage...'*

Suddenly, Sara was startled out of her tropical daydream by a blood curdling scream. A woman's voice. Sara's head craned towards their neighbor's home, after hearing a loud "No!" piercing the air.

Dropping her spade, she ran quickly next door. Tentatively, peering through the open front door Sara asked "Is everything okay in there?" Hearing sobbing coming from the kitchen, she stepped gingerly inside to the heart-wrenching sound. Lady Lee, their neighbor, was lying face down on the kitchen floor. There was a small pool of dried blood near her head.

A woman kneeled by her side with sounds of moaning. Wiping away the tears from her forearm, she gazed up at Sara, mustering, "I'm afraid she's gone. I've been trying to call Lee for the past couple days. I'm her sister, Miriam."

Clinging onto the body, she breathed, "Even though I live across the state, we've stayed close. Called nearly every day."

Ben was now standing in the kitchen doorway, "I heard the scream," he said, "I've already phoned 911."

Sara knew about Lee's sister, 'Miriam the RN', so thought better than to check for vital signs.

Instinctively though, Ben kneeled down, looking around the room, " She must have had a stroke while standing at the sink," he said. "She would have hit her head with quite an impact on the tile after falling. Tragic..."

After the ambulance and coroner had left, Sara and Ben stayed to comfort Miriam, "I'll boil some tea," Sara said softly.

Sitting in an old needlepoint chair, Marium fidgeted while searching through a big purse. "I knew it!" she bristled, "'I told her not to take it." Glazing over, all was still.

Ben and Sara sat motionless on the old couch, clasping hands together, fastening their eyes on her for clarity.

"A week ago, Lee called me about taking this mRNA injection they call the vaccine." Miriam held up a slip of paper she found in the purse. "This vaccination card shows she took the shot two days ago. I warned her—I warned her."

"The Covid spike proteins must have penetrated the blood-brain barrier almost immediately, causing the stroke when she arrived home." Ben suggested clinically.

Sara squeezed his hand interjecting, "Unfortunately, we're leaving for a medical conference ourselves in a few days, but please let us know if there's anything we can do to help. Would you like us to pray for you and your sister right now?"

"Well," Miriam relaxed now. "Our parents did take us to church sometimes. Yes—please; Lee would have liked that."

The night before flying to the Island conference, Sara woke suddenly, "I dreamt they were going to try something, like separating us at the airport," she nudged Ben awake.

Groggy, he had her repeat the dream twice. "Maybe it's a warning about the injections." Ben scribbled a note to grab his University Lab ID, in the morning, before heading to the airport. *Just in case...*

Chapter 8

"Having been 'Born Again' not of corruptible seed, but incorruptible, through the Word of God," 1st Peter 1:23.

At the ticket counter in the morning, the Copa Air agent said something sternly in Spanish. Ben and Sara looked at each other knowingly, after hearing *'Vacuna Passport.'*

"They want our vaccine passport cards," Ben frowned. "Maybe its because our connecting flight is in Central America." With the heads up from Sara's dream, he held up his medical lanyard from around his neck.

"No es obligatorio, mi esposo es investigador medico, y recibio' vacunas cuando eran bebes," Sara said.

The ticket agent looked bewildered, but nodded and handed them the boarding passes.

"What did you say to him," Ben asked dodging the crowd.

"I told him you were *Medical* and we were both vaccinated as babies—then you showed him your medical lanyard card.

"Well whatever works," he replied with relief, "I'm sticking with you—where did you learn such *'Bueno Espanol?'*

"Remember my mission trips to Rosarita, with the youth group? That, and *Cinco Anos Española en Escuala.*"

"What?" he puzzled, "Five years with a fish?"

"That's *Pescado*," she poked him. "I had five years in school. Maybe you slept through your Spanish classes."

"Si!" he grinned.

On the plane, masks were required, but they found a *loophole*. "No one bugs us when we are eating," he analyzed.

While Sara napped, Ben studied how the World Economic Forum would be meeting in Davos, Switzerland, with the World Health Organization and some of the most powerful elite in the world to further their One World Agenda. *Quite a contrast to our Medical Freedom conference meeting at the same time*, he garnered.

"The flight and customs agents were a breeze," Sara walked briskly to the baggage claim.

"Yes, but they were messing with us at the Airlines check-in counter. There are no travel requirements for the shots, tests, or even masks here."

After arriving at the hotel, hosting the conference, they took a long nap before exploring. The Island Resort seemed even nicer than they expected. Lush tropical grounds were filled with bright red hibiscus flowers and birds of paradise. Fresh scents of jasmine flooded the air. They noticed the large pool area was virtually empty. It seemed as though with the lockdowns, they would have the resort all to themselves.

Quite a conundrum, Ben thought, *here we are enjoying so freely, while the rest of the world is behind bars.*

Returning to their seventh-floor suite, a large veranda gave sweeping views of the turquoise Caribbean waters. Sara commented, "Sort of makes you feel guilty, doesn't it?"

"Not in the slightest," Ben laughed, while searching his suitcase for a swimsuit.

For Ben, mornings were filled with lectures and breakout sessions. Replete with lively discussion on the recent *Medical Tyranny*, as many doctors and scientists labeled the pandemic protocols.

Afternoons were spent walking, snorkeling and sailing.

At dusk, the beach boardwalk was filled with festive lights and savory aromas of the Mayan cuisine. It flooded out of every open-air kitchen. No one wore masks or seemed very concerned.

One local restaurant owner spoke in a heavy accent explaining, "We don't have time to watch TV—we don't know to be sick," he laughed.

Another young busboy simply said, "Not possible to be sick. I have a wife and baby at home to feed." Sara and Ben enjoyed passing out their Little Bibles in Spanish, to the locals who were so thankful.

In the opening meetings, many noted doctors spoke about the technical aspects of mRNA vaccines and their pitfalls. Several knew about the toxins Ben discovered in The Cole Report. He also shared some of his own grim discoveries.

Not many had begun to see the bigger depopulation agenda, or the spiritual aspects of these injections. That the seed of humanity was in danger; that mankind remaining *Made in the Image of God* was of greatest concern.

The convention panel began with an organizer, Dr. Gold. "Let's face it, these are bioweapons. It would be shameful if we do not sound the alarm."

Dr. Robert Malone, the inventor of the mRNA, in the vaccinations, adamantly opposed their use, saying: "The Pharmaceutical company's own internal documents reveal that the mRNA should never have been approved for emergency use. They will cause harm at every age level."

"They falsified all of their so-called studies," Dr. Gold replied. "They're paying off the government and media too."

At the same time, the Freedom Doctors were meeting in Cozumel, the WEF—World Economic Forum, Summit was meeting in Davos Switzerland. It featured a record turnout from many of the most powerful government and corporate officials. Several doctors watched the opening one evening, on a link sent by Ben's nephew.

Davos executive chairman Klaus Schnob called for all world leaders to unite, by addressing global issues such as the pandemic, climate change, trade, and economic disruption. He emphasized that a One-World Government must form as soon as possible.

"The impact of the Fourth Industrial Revolution accelerates global change in a much more comprehensive and faster way than the previous industrial revolutions,"

Schnob said to the assembled world leaders. He emphasized the use of mass vaccinations worldwide.

Ben realized it was by no accident that Schnob referred to the "Fourth Industrial Revolution," after reading Daniel 7:

'The Fourth Beast—there will be a fourth kingdom upon the earth which will be different from all the kingdoms; it will devour the whole earth, tread it down, and crush it.'

They called it *The Great Reset,* but this was calculated. Schnob described the pandemic as a rare opportunity. "The world will have damage done to our economies and societies by COVID-19. "We must seize on this for global control."

"You will own nothing and be happy!" was another catchphrase bantered about by the uncaring elite. Another one of their younger spokesmen, was a gay man named, Yuvale Ahab Herari. The Israeli professor, promoted Transhumanism, casually suggesting, "There will shortly be an *End to Homo Sapiens.*"

One Messianic Rabbi responded saying:

THE FINAL SEED

"The leaders who seek God's glory and know that their mandate comes from Him, are successful and bring light into the world. Others reject the Lord. They inevitably bring darkness into the world. *If Klaus Schnob really wanted to help people, its simple. The answer is written in the Bible. They are rich while others are poor and starving in the world. Do they care about people? No—they worship themselves."*

At Davos, numerous heads of state and public officials attended. There were finance ministers, central bank governors, heads of global organizations, the United Nations, the International Monetary Fund, and the World Trade Organization. There were 600 CEOs and 1000 executives from

700 of the world's largest corporations attending.

Hundreds of private jets wasted fuel for the elite to mix with leaders and celebrities from around the world. They used the pandemic narrative, talk of global climate crisis and world wars, to fuel their wicked plans.

The Global elite were already making billions from the crisis they created, according to the conference lawyer, Ben had met.

At dinner that night, Sara imagined the Davos leaders eating caviar while sipping on aged cognac and bottles of wine, costing thousands of dollars each. She became flushed at the thought. *It makes my blood boil for the children.*

In a polar opposite, Ben's Medical Freedom Conference, meeting on Isla Cozumel, was being held in the quaint banquet room of the El Cid, an older Mayan resort by the sea. The tall glass windows afforded a spectacular vista of the Caribbean. Ben gazed at a passing catamaran. *Sometimes makes it a little difficult to concentrate on lab findings.*

Dr. Derek Stein, a clinical lab scientist, took to the podium to report their results: "We tested 1500 Covid samples supposedly positive with virus. My lab team did the testing through post postulates and observation, using a scanning electron microscope. We found no Covid in any of the 1500 samples. We found that all of the 1500 samples had either Influenza A or Influenza B, but not a single case of Covid.

We *did not* use the bogus PCR—the Polymerase Chain Reaction test. We then sent the remainder of the samples to Cornell, Stanford, and several other University labs, who all found the same results; *No Covid!*

"We have now come to the firm conclusion after all our research and lab work, Covid-19 is imaginary and fictitious. The flu is called Covid. Most of those dying are now deceased because of prior health conditions, *Comorbidities.*

After taking the shots or tests, with a weakened immune system, they die from cancer, stroke, heart attacks, diabetes, or emphysema. Hospital protocols, like ventilation, or using drugs like Remdesivir, helps kill them.

Dr. Stein elaborated, "So far, not one researcher, or scientist worldwide has discovered a single viable sample of Covid-19 to work with. The seven universities testing these 1500 samples, are now suing the CDC for *Covid-19 fraud.* The flu is called Covid to create a *'Plandemic'* filled with government lies, fear and death. The goal is to have everyone on the planet take these nefarious poison injections," he grimaced.

On a morning conference break, Ben took a brisk walk along the ocean pier. Several of the doctors were discussing the cruise ships—in quarantine—anchored out in the Bay.

The mainstream media had reported many on cruise ships worldwide had Covid sickness. Now on his seaside walk, Ben overheard a doctor from the conference say, "They are concealing the 5G microwave radiation in those large round white balls on top of the cruise ships—There!" He pointed up to several hidden towers. "What they call 'Covid' is most likely radiation sickness."

In one of the days breakout sessions, Dr. Northrup and Dr. Madej reported they had contacted the fertility clinics, who said they've never seen anything like it.

"The sperm of inoculated men do not swim, and the eggs of inoculated women do not turn into embryos, Christine Northrup, the renowned OBGYN reported.

"And those that do turn into embryos, have a huge amount of contamination with non-organic material," our colleague, Dr. Carrie Madej, found.

Doctor Northrup pointed up to the projection screen; "According to the First New England Journal of medicine study, then comparing current raw data, it proves that 80% of the women who get the shot in the first and second trimester, have an 80% miscarriage rate. The miscarriage rate Baseline was one out of six. It's now 7 to 8 times that amount."

In another key message, Dr. Sean Brooks, an older physician from Oxford stated, "Dr. Robert Malone, who created the messenger RNA in vaccines, said no one should ever take these jabs ever, under any circumstance, whatsoever. He created it, and he says 'Don't ever do it.' Let me give you three reasons why. First, you dramatically decrease the immune system by over 35% with the shots.

"If you take booster shots, you will die with a lower mortality. That's it. When someone takes a flu shot, they now contain the messenger RNA, and will shorten lives." The Oxford physician was not one to mince words.

"The second reason is *'Antibody Dependent Enhancement.'* It tricks the entire body into believing the cell eating the pathogen is doing so, when it isn't. It ends up leading to what is termed a 'cytokine storm.' This causes organ failure.

There's no stopping this process once begun. No number of pharmaceutical drugs will stop it.

"The third reason is blood clotting. Many taking the shots now show signs of clotting. You don't believe me? – you can find out for yourself with a simple test. It's called a D-dimer test. It detects blood clotting at a microscopic level. They are cutting full blood clots out of people right now as I'm speaking to you. Millions are already dying from these *'Clot Shots.'* The government, the pharmaceuticals and the media are doing everything in their power to cover it up.

"So, to the parents who are considering jabbing their own children—you may sterilize them permanently," he sighed.

"They are sterilizing humans. We need to do the right thing, and depopulate those who are promoting this evil agenda." Dr. Brooks, gazed askance at the crowd and walked to the edge of the stage, literally throwing his hands up into the air—"Let's stop them!" he finished speaking, peering directly into a video camera.

Later that day, up in the room, Ben mentioned all the evils discovered from the shots. Sara replied, "Sounds like you need to unwind. I already reserved a couple of bikes for a sunset ride around the island."

Minutes later they were cruising in the bike lane by the scenic Caribbean Sea. Both bicycles sported thick blue tires. Hers held a pink basket attached in front, with tasty treats.

"We have the whole Island to ourselves," she led the way. Shortly, they had circumnavigated to the windward side of the Isla. The larger waves danced high in the late afternoon sunlight, effervescing a spectrum of colors; shining with emerald, lavender and gold. "The tips of the waves are glowing!" she beamed.

"I've never seen anything so beautiful," Ben replied, "other than you…"

"Oh Ben," she reached for his hand, pulling him off the bike towards the waves.

"You want us to jump in with our clothes on?"

Momentarily, they paused in the white sand at the edge of the sea, listening to the pounding surf. The snow-white foam crested to their knees. Without a care, Ben threw off his Hawaiian shirt plunging headlong into the turquoise waters. Sara followed eagerly in her bright floral sundress.

In the ocean swell, thoughts of messenger RNA, and spike proteins were washed away by the stirring waters.

Back inside the conference room, the following day, a Pediatrician from Canada, Dr. Rosalyn Jones reported more grim news: "As doctors, we have to balance the risk of a disease with the risk of a dangerous experimental 'vaccine.' The risk of contracting this virus almost disappears with children. Covid vaccination risks conversely are higher the younger the age. The shots are more deadly for the children.

"The AstraZeneca for example has been withdrawn in many countries, because of dangerous blood clots found. The Pfizer shot has been linked to myocarditis, or inflammation of the heart, which will become a death sentence itself.

"In younger people, the toxins accumulate in the testes and ovaries often causing infertility. The risk of the vaccine is greater than the risk of the virus itself. Please! I'm a grandmother," she pleaded with a softer tone, "We cannot sacrifice our children and the next generation."

One key speaker at the conference was Dr. Zelenko, who had attended President Trump while recovering from what the doctor labeled a "bio weapon." Bearded and bushy haired, the famous Jewish doctor reported using Ivermectin, Zinc, Vitamins C, D, a daily aspirin and then a natural Hydroxychloroquine, weekly after the treatment.

"We've shared this treatment method with many of you in the medical community, and I'm happy to report that we have successfully treated over thirty-five thousand Covid patients!" he beamed.

In the afternoon, a Professor of Botany and plant science, from Trinity Western, in B.C., lectured with a warning about the food supply. The shaggy haired younger man turned his back to the attendees, while addressing a large video screen filled with scientific data.

In a nasal monotone, he sounded, "The worldwide campaign to vaccinate every man, woman and child on earth is headed straight for your dinner plate! A group of researchers from UC Riverside and San Diego are researching ways to turn your groceries into mRNA vaccines, to spread Coronavirus spike proteins throughout the food chain. They want to fool the world population and those resisting these experimental vaccines. They call them the 'vaccine hesitant.'

"This experiment could lead to a new vaccine paradigm in which big pharma has complete control over the food supply. Is this why Billy Bates is the major investor in genetically modified crops? He's spearheading the vaccine roll out. He's been buying up most of the organic farms across the United States. He's been acquiring them from the start of the Covid pandemic, without any oversight from the Department of Agriculture, or media. Bates is now the owner of the majority of farmland in the country."

The young botanist turned and searched the faces in the room now asking several pertinent questions. "Will the food supply be made up of worm food for people and tainted with GMO/mRNA seeds? Will it be used to administer vaccinations? Are we headed for famine as the Bible warns?"

Ben spotted Sara watching from the back and waved her over to sit with him.

"Using a grant from the National Science Foundation, experiments on lettuce and spinach and corn, have already begun with the intention of developing a new species of greens that vaccinate people daily and will be considered less invasive than a needle shoved into the arm.

"A hospital in Ottawa is already testing the first prototype. This edible vaccine expresses viral antigens inside the spinach and lettuce plants. At a deeper level, they want to vaccinate people without them even knowing it. People are reluctant to take further shots, so now they're going to turn healthy healing foods into bio-warfare, or use a nano-patch. The globalists want Covid vaccines to proliferate throughout the entire food chain; forever altering God-given natural seeds to toxic ones. "We have to remember compassion for the innocent in this."

The Botanist flashed bright blue eyes, "Let's face it—a GMO tomato tastes terrible, There's no flavor in any of them. The seeds are eliminated in many these fruits too. They don't want anyone to have an organic garden, or grow their own healthy foods.

"They also plan to vaccinate the animals with mRNA. Thanksgiving dinner will never be the same," he snickered. The young botanist finished with a plea: "Pray for divine intervention!"

This young man obviously has a strong faith, Ben discerned.

Sitting in on the session, Sara whispered in Ben's ear, "Maybe we can take this young man to dinner and encourage him."

"Let's not order any salads though," Ben quipped, gently squeezing her hand.

The next morning, a prominent U.S. Senator, Paul Rand, gave a televised message live from his Congressional office. As a former surgeon himself, he headed a committee investigating the pandemic. They had discovered the head of the National Health Institute, Dr. Fausti, was diverting federal funding. Under a cover called *'Gain of Function,'* they ostensibly appropriated funds and provided a lab created virus, to set-up a clinic in Wuhan, China.

Fausti, had been caught lying to Congress several times, while under oath. Even with this, Senator Rand complained he could not press formal charges for contempt of Congress.

"Our select committee is taking on the industrial pharmaceutical and national medical agencies that receive billions in government funding," Senator Rand stated. "It's proceeding slowly with the opposition—its a *'Pay for Play'* system, with the pharmaceutical industry. Most all members of Congress take the dirty money. Most legislators are compromised by lobbyists and big business interests.

"The courts may be a better alternative for remedy. This goes to the First Amendment and freedom of speech," his banter slowed, "I was accosted last week outside my office; I was *attacked*." The Senator held up a bandaged wrist to the camera.

"There's a smear campaign in the media for anyone with opposing views, such as myself, or presumably your group.

"As a former heart surgeon, myself, I can tell you that I believe many taking the experimental vaccinations will be developing mitochondria and auto-immune diseases, from the spike proteins released by mRNA. Let us keep pressing on to expose this tragedy no matter what. God bless you all!"

On the last day of the conference, the event organizer called Ben early, "We had a special guest scheduled to speak at the morning session. His plane from Europe is running late. Would you please fill in with an update on any of your findings?"

Without preparation, Ben was hesitant. Then with an urging in his spirit, he agreed to share what was on his heart. Skipping breakfast was a usual pattern, so he spent an hour jotting down ideas and researching his own notebook.

Taking the stand promptly at nine AM, Ben shared some new research and tried to remain calm. Noticing an older gentleman watching from the wings of the stage, Ben's blood began pumping. It was Dr. Luc Montagnier. The French virologist had received the Noble Prize for discovering the immunodeficiency virus, HIV. He was one of the first scientists to say that the Covid virus was artificially made in a lab.

Departing from his notes, Ben moved in the spirit. "This week we heard these are not vaccines. They are DNA changing with auto-immune deficiencies and infertility."

"When we studied all of these structures under an electron microscope, the Vials contained graphene Nano ribbons, Darpahydrogels, self-assembling Nano-tech, parasites, chimera DNA and Luciferase, for possible marking and tracking.

"The CDC and FDA disregard natural immunity now. Where's the funding to study these toxins? All week long we have heard about side-effects and physical ailments and even death from the injections.

"We need to question why they're installing so many 5G transmitters, originally designed as a weapons system? Why are they spraying the skies with toxic metals?

"What we have not discussed is the *Why*? We haven't processed the spiritual implications." Ben paused realizing that every eye was now riveted on his next words.

Collecting his thoughts, he proceeded methodically, "Listen, my grandfather was on the front lines in WWII, as a soldier at the Battle of the Bulge. At the end of the war, they assisted the Jews who were still alive at Dachau. In my youth, I often heard Grandpa say, *'The walking dead were coming out of the death camps for miles.'* It really stuck with me. They were like skeletons, he said. How could anyone do such a thing? There were the dreaded Nazi's, but there were also thousands of doctors, scientists and nurses involved."

Ben hung his head, "For a believer, the God-fearing Jews were the chosen people of God; from Abraham, Isaac and Jacob. From King David, who slew the Nephilim giant, Goliath, to the Messiah, Jesus. The Holocaust was genocide, it was de-population. We have to consider it—is this not happening again?" Pausing, he reached for a remote clicker.

"Normally, I would be showing you our lab findings on the screens here, but I think we have established the deadly toxicity in these shots. What you see here are photos of concentration camps. These are *not* the death camps from World War two—these are Covid camps. They're happening *right now*. In China, over one million people are interred. Australia, Canada and in the U.S., FEMA camps are reportedly being built. Listen—are they arresting those refusing to take the mRNA injections?" he asked frowning.

"We have to realize they will blame the deaths from the shots on the unvaccinated!"

Taking a deep breath, Ben processed his own impromptu statement, *'They will blame the deaths from these shots on the unvaccinated.'* "You know I'm an Epi-geneticist at heart," he stammered. "Giving a talk like this really isn't my area..."

"Keep going—you're doing fine!" Dr. Zelenko shouted out in encouragement. Ben turned his head towards the sound. Dr. Zelenko was standing next to Dr. Montagnier, waiting in the wings of the stage.

"Have you ever heard of *The Georgia Guidestones*?" Ben asked hesitantly. "My wife and I live right over the border from where they are in Georgia. These granite monoliths are often referred to as 'America's Stonehenge'. But after seeing them in person, most faithful people call them *'The Devils Ten Commandments.'*

On the large Video screen Ben posted a photo with the writings from one of the tall monoliths. "The first 'commandment' says it all." It read: Maintain Humanity under 500,000,000 in perpetual balance with nature. "Do you see this?" Ben spoke softly, scanning the room.

"They call it conspiracy, but we have witnessed these words first hand; Maintain Humanity under 500,000,000.... So is this truly their goal—to reduce the World's population by over ninety percent?" Several in the crowd answered in the affirmative.

"One final thought," Ben spoke more confidently now. "In Belgium, they convened the Nuremberg trials after the second World War. They prosecuted many scientists and those responsible for their evil experiments on humans. Many of them were hung for their evil deeds. Maybe its time we begin these prosecutions again," he ended solemnly.

One person began to clap in a steady cadence. The lone sound was coming from Sara's direction. Then rescuing the awkward moment, Dr. Luc Montagnier and Dr. Zelenko, both began clapping, coming from stage side, to the podium.

With sudden assertion, each grabbed one of Ben's arms from either side, lifting theirs all together, forming a victory salute. The whole crowd instantly sprung to its feet with applause. Ben became flushed, as the rhythmic effect of prolonged applause seemed to hold him hostage on the platform.

As Ben departed the podium, eighty-seven-year-old, Dr. Luc Montagnier, gave Ben a pat on the back, switching places.

Dr. Luc gave a short talk to wrap things up. He spoke in a thick French accent, "This Coronavirus, SARS COV-2, was manufactured and leaked from a Wuhan lab in China with HIV, AIDS DNA." The famous geneticist had received Noble Prize for discovering HIV and autoimmune-deficiencies.

Dr. Luc shared how there would be dire consequences for mass vaccination, "Lifespans will be shortened dramatically."

A stern look came over his rugged face, "I warn you physicians responsible for the future of mankind, if any of you continue to administer these shots to trusting patients."

"For any of you taking these gene-changing vaccines, go and take an AIDS test. The results may surprise you. Then sue your government..."

Dr. Montagnier's final statement to the group well summed up the tenor of their conference: "These are *NOT* vaccines; these are deadly poisons!"

With the conference finally ending, Dr. Gold, the organizer, asked all of the speakers to return to the stage. "We must stay united against medical tyranny," she stated defiantly.

Then on behalf of the members, Dr. Robert Malone, the mRNA inventor, presented the consensus of the group:

Ten-point Summit Health Declaration:

1. We declare and the data confirms that the COVID experimental genetic therapy injections must end.

2. We declare doctors should *not* be blocked from providing life-saving medical treatment.

3. We declare the state of national emergency, which facilitates corruption and extends the pandemic, should be immediately terminated.

4. We declare medical privacy should never again be violated, and all travel and social restrictions must cease.

5. We declare masks are not and have never been effective protection against an airborne respiratory virus.

6. We declare funding and research must be established for vaccination damage, death and suffering.

7. We declare no opportunity should be denied, including education, career, military service or medical treatment, over unwillingness to take an injection.

8. We declare that first amendment violations and medical censorship by government, technology and media companies should cease, and the Bill of Rights be upheld.

9. We declare that Pfizer, Moderna, BioNTech, Janssen, Astra Zeneca, and their enablers, withheld and willfully omitted safety and effectiveness information from patients and physicians, and should be immediately indicted for fraud.

10. We declare government and medical agencies are held accountable to the full extent of the law and Nuremberg code.

Heading home from the Island, on a ferry to the Yucatan Peninsula, they were informed that the United States had enacted new stringent testing requirements for entry. All those without the shots would need a negative Covid test to fly.

Returning to Playa del Carmen on their way to the airport, most all of the conference attendees were scrambling, trying to find a non-nasal Rapid Antigen test. None wanted to take the PCR. The researchers had analyzed that Covid symptoms often developed afterward. Even worse, the deep penetration into the nostril, from the swab, could break the blood-brain barrier, possibly putting the toxic materials into brain tissue itself.

Now in Playa del Carmen, Ben and Sara visited several clinics. Finally, there was one willing to do an Antigen test. Refusing to have the swab placed up the nose, or in the cheek Ben pulled out a large Peso bill showing it to the clinician.

"We're hoping to give you a little extra '*Propina*,' a *tip* for all your trouble for fitting us in your schedule," he mentioned. Sara translated to the Spanish speaking nurse.

Reaching for two plastic cups, from a bag, Ben motioned to the nurse, dressed in a bright blue uniform. Then they both spit into a cup and Ben pointed for the nurse to retrieve each test sample by dipping a Q-tip right into the cup.

"I can't believe that worked," Sara nudged him in the shuttle to the Cancun Airport. "Where did you find those cups?"

"They were poolside at the resort."

"Ugh—hope you washed them first.
"Sure, they were sterilized with alcohol," he laughed.

THE FINAL SEED

On the plane ride home, Ben read a handout from Dr. Vladimir Zelenko. His short message was riveting:

1. Covid-19 is an engineered virus that caused Global psychosis. Psychosis caused people to Vax.
2. Vax is for eugenics, surveillance and genetic manipulation to corrupt the seed of man.
3. The Globalist agenda is population reduction, enslavement, altering what it means to be human. Globalists don't believe in God, or afterlife, and believe that human consciousness disappears with death.
4. Globalists fear death, and believe they can create an inorganic/organic hybrid form with 'AI' and that human consciousness can be downloaded.
5. Globalists believe they have evolved to a higher level of consciousness and can evade death.
6. Globalists believe the rest of humanity are a waste of resources and population should be culled by 90%.
7. Solution is to choose God over the Globalist;

Know we are in a real War:

WAR (P)
S (P) EED

Chapter 9

Arriving home from the airport in the dark, Sara grabbed a flashlight from the glovebox in the car and ran to check on the garden, "It must have rained a lot while we were gone," she called out, "just two weeks—and the tomatoes already need poles to hold up the vines!"

"That's great hon—let's buy some more organic seeds," Ben responded, rolling their suitcases inside.

The next day, Sara checked for seeds online, "they're removing the organic ones—I can't find them anywhere..."

After some fresh brewed coffee and oatmeal, Ben called his nephew on the encrypted line, relating details from the conference.

Marshal answered, "I've been trying to reach you at the conference, after hearing they possibly planted someone down there. Did you notice a taller blonde man with an extremely close-cropped haircut?"

"Not off the top of my head, but I'll check on the videos they were filming."

"The Bates Foundation is buying up every organic farm he can get his hands on in the country," his nephew confirmed. I'm sure they'll be switching them over to GMO seeds right away.

Ben mentioned the talk he heard at the conference, from the young Botanist, reporting about the mRNA experiments being conducted to introduce the vaccinations into the food chain. "They want people and food genetically modified."

"No wonder he's buying up all the organic farms," Marshal recoiled. "All of the organic seeds too."

"Is it true they have a Seed Bank located in Iceland?"

"It's so idiotic Uncle Ben! They built this impenetrable structure, but I heard it's already slipping into the ice. Maybe they didn't really want to save the seeds—like they've been telling some of us—probably wanted to destroy them all along. He and his cronies might destroy every natural seed left and poison all the soil, if someone doesn't stop them," Marshal moaned.

That night Ben discovered a report by Dr. Don Davis, a Biochemist from a University in Texas. The study revealed that most all of the minerals were depleted from the soil.

Plants, animals and scientists cannot make minerals. Over a sixty percent mineral content in the soil is essential for health. Toxic chemicals, such as Roundup, or Glyphosate had poisoned the earth. Most of the farm land was stripped of minerals and nutrients. Gone was the calcium, magnesium and zinc and dozens of other trace minerals.

The genetically modified seeds had proliferated. Pesticides and herbicides sown right into the plants, not only killed the bugs, they killed the good bacteria in the soil. *Would these same toxins woven into the seeds and plants eventually cause cancers and kill people too?* Ben wondered.

On the first morning back in the lab, Ben viewed the strange memo in his hands. Several calls had come in with ominous sounding messages while they were at the conference. He listened to the them for *'Umpteenth Time,'* as his Carolina grandma used to say, in her heavy drawl. Then it dawned on him. *These are from a federal government agency—one of those covert ones.*

Tending the garden was cooler in the late afternoon. Sara took the time to meditate on the miracles of God, so evident in the tiny seeds, sprouting into edible plants or trees bearing fruit. The Lord had given her a beautiful organic garden now. Maybe her seed was not to bear children, but she certainly had a green thumb.

Her new neighbor, Miriam, often chatted from her own nearby garden. *What a blessing to have such a sweet new friend, who shares both gardening tips and faith.*

Miriam mentioned warning others, as a nurse, albeit privately, about the injections and evil hospital protocols; "My Sisters death from the serpents shot will not be in vain!"

Ben will be home any minute, Sara considered. *Better get something on the stove. And there's enough greens for a fresh organic salad.*

Right on cue Ben sped into the driveway honking the horn.

Leaning out the car window he called, "Are you ready for this?"

"For what?" Suddenly, a large dog jumped out of the vehicle barking and running towards Sara. Bracing herself, the dog lept with excitement, in her direction.

Sara was quick, but not quick enough, falling backward into the soft garden bed. Both of them began laughing.

"Oh Ben, he's huge!"

"Your dad thought we could use a well-trained guard dog, with everything going on. It's an Akita. They're known for such things."

Helping Sara back to her feet, she asked, "What's his name?"

"Well the 'he is a she'"...

"Kin—it means golden."

"Then while petting through the thick fur of the Akita with her garden gloved hand, Sara lowered her tone. "Good girl, good girl, but I might call you 'Kimmy' instead."

"Sure that's a first for this breed."

Miriam, following the noise, peered from around the corner of their garden shed. The dog gave a deep growl. Sara held tightly to the collar.

"See? Your new protector," Ben nodded.

"Come meet our newest family member," Sara called to Miriam. "I don't think she will bite."

"Just keep smiling and saying 'Good girl—good girl,'" Ben petted through the thick fur.

That evening, Newsmax reported Senator Paul Rand was in the hospital fighting for his life. He'd been attacked over the weekend in his own backyard in Virginia. Details were sketchy, but one reliable news source reported the assailant had recently rented the home next door. He had reportedly worked for both the NSA and NIH.

Later that night, the OAN Network did a report on the *Deep State*. "Our health agencies with DARPA at the Pentagon, are behind mandating vaccinations and ID cards for everyone," the reporter shook his head.

A former FBI Agent revealed, "Any opposing view is considered '*Anti-American*,' and is deplatformed by the shadow government-controlled media."

At sunrise, Sara found Ben sitting quietly in the garden on the bench he had made for her. "It's beautiful," she cooed.

Admiring the tall plants, Ben interjected, "Yes, it's a beautiful garden. I think we will have enough for all of our neighbors."

"I was speaking about the nice bench you made me—I love you Mr. Strickland!"

"I love you too sweetie—together we can get through anything."

"I'm so thankful lady Lee's sister decided to move in next door. Her garden's really coming along too. We have a lot in common." Her husband sat quietly. "You seem so pensive..."

"I've been on the dedicated line this morning. While we were away, a government investigator kept calling work asking for me."

"Did they say why?"

"Talked with them this morning and they want to meet me. They were asking about Dr. Cole." It weighed on Ben's mind as they sat holding hands on the bench, but he never held anything back from his wife, "When I called Doctor Cole, someone answered saying he's gone missing."

"Dr. Cole's missing?—this isn't adding up, Ben."

"That's not all, hundreds of the most noted Integrative Medicine, M.D.'s and Holistic doctors, have died this year," he groaned. "All were opposed to the shots. And researchers exposing the evils are being prosecuted."

"That's beyond suspicious." Sara had a way of furrowing her brow. "Do we need to be concerned for our safety, Ben? I saw one of the online doctors showing pictures of quarantine camps right here in the States. One of them said the government purchased guillotines for FEMA. It's all so hard to believe."

"My dad used to quote a Robert Frost poem to me." Ben lifted his brows, slowly recalling the poem: "*If you can keep your head when all about you others are losing theirs—then you will be a man my son.*"

"That's not funny, Ben!"

They took some quiet time together praying for guidance.

In a moment, Sara broke the silence, "Do you remember our meeting the lawyer from Washington D.C. at the conference?"

"Not many Jesus followers are attorneys," Ben replied, "hard guy to forget..."

"He mentioned helping anyone that was in trouble—think we have his business card inside the house."

"Your *Holy intuition* comes in handy," he hugged her.

Before bed, he sent a short email, to the D.C. Lawyer: *'Appreciated meeting you at the conference. Several federal investigators have been hounding me, will you consider helping?'* Ben included details about the Cole Report and the government contact details from the messages.

Clearing his computer, Ben was ready to head upstairs to bed, when the message board suddenly lit up on his screen. Marked *'Urgent'* it appeared to be an email from Dr Cole. *"There's not much time left. You are one of the only ones remaining who received the package. Must keep going. Genetic sequencing for the bio virus was compromised from the start of current pandemic. The genetic virus was stolen. Sent through NIH to Wuhan lab with U.S. funding. For use in the manner of our CH Lab manufactured viruses for the 'V's listed in report. Refer to Report, Section 9!"*

Before Ben could finish reading, the last sentence began to disappear. Letter by letter, the words disappeared rapidly *backwards* from the last line. As if an invisible hand controlled his board now, a finger on the delete button. Frantically, Ben worked to retrieve the email, vanishing before his eyes. It was not to be recovered.

For the longest time, Ben shuffled about the office, rolling in his chair, contemplating what he had just witnessed on the screen. Sara would already be fast asleep upstairs.

Finally, closing his eyes, Ben prayed; *Lord, let me never forget You in the midst. Show me what I need to know here.* In an instant, calculations concerning the genome flooded his head. A picture of a double stranded helix forming in a womb and then a third strand woven from without in a robotic fashion.

Recalling the words in Cole's email, *'In the manner of those Lab-Made Viruses,'* Ben now lifted a package fastened under his desk.

Opening the contents, he found the page he was looking for. It read:

96

AIDS US-Patent 5676977

H1N1 US-Patent 8835624

Ebola US-Patent 20120251502

Swine Flu US-Patent CA2741523 A1

BSE US-Patent 0070031450 A1

ZIKA ATTC VR-84 (Rockefeller Foundation)

SARS US-Patent 7897744 & 8506968

CORONAVIRUS US-Patent 10130701

Writing on the bottom of the page, Ben neatly added:

Bates, Mycro Soft—Cov Crypto/ Patent Number: WO2020-060606 (666)

'For every man-made virus, comes a corresponding 'vaccine.'

Tomorrow research the genome numeric values in Lab.' Copying the page, he tucked it neatly in his briefcase before heading upstairs.

Early in the morning, the ringing from Ben's cell startled them awake. "For starters, they want a list of everyone you've given the Cole report," his D.C. attorney began. "Its part Military; a DCIS investigation."

Ben responded by side-stepping the Cole Report request, providing a verbal laundry list of the doctors disappearing, or dying in mysterious ways. He mentioned Senator Rand was most likely one of the latest victims.

"Would the Pentagon be involved in this sort of thing?"

"In this town, you never know..." the lawyer paused. "In better news, we heard from Rand's office this morning and he's going to pull through. He's losing one lung, though."

"Sorry to hear that—but glad he's pulling through okay."

The lawyer went on, "With your permission, we can take this on pro-bono—several of the doctors banded together and gave us a nice stipend for cases such as yours."

"Thank you—thank you for the representation," Ben replied gratefully. "We'll pray for Senator Rand's recovery."

"I've known Rand a long time. His committee is already sending out several more subpoenas," the lawyer finished.

On his way to work, Ben met with Pastor A.J. to seek *wise counsel*, and fill him in on the details from the conference. Over breakfast, Ben shared the predicament he was in after the call from the government agent.

"FBI - CIA?" Pastor A.J. asked.

"Something like that—we met a faithful attorney at the conference, from Washington D.C., who offered to help."

After a short prayer, A.J. lit up, "While you were gone, I began to weave a lot of information from your research into my sermons. Most of it lined up with scripture and end-times prophecies. With your advice, we began broadcasting the messages live online. There's been a tremendous response."

"That's wonderful news, Pastor!"

"Got that right—anything to get out the Gospel like this. We're starting a new Series calling it 'Prophecy Now.'" A.J. lifted a cloth napkin from his front breast pocket, wiping his brow.

"My oldest teenage son has been sharing the messages live online. He said the online video last week had over half a million views. Unfortunately, the video was removed immediately," A.J. grimaced. "But I did close with the Gospel message."

"The most important of all," Ben smiled.

A.J. spoke boldly for the other tables to hear:

"Jesus died for our sins on the cross. On the third day he rose again from the tomb and conquered death, so that those who believe in him can have eternal life. He ascended to heaven and sits at the right hand of God the Father Almighty and will return again with his angels to gather his saints from the four corners of the Earth. And so we shall forever be with the Lord. That is the Gospel, he beamed. It never gets old!"

"Now that's what were called to share," Ben nodded.

"*Gospel* means: *Good News*!" A.J. bellowed. A young server perked up her ears nearby and gave them a knowing smile.

An idea came to Ben's mind, "You mentioned they removed your online message, '*but there's more than one way to skin a cat*,' my grandpa used to say."

"Bad thing if you're a cat."

Ben continued undaunted. "Try streaming the sermons online 'Live' and then have people switch directly to the church website after you begin, for the weightier content the beast will censure."

"That just—might—work," A.J. nodded.

At dawn the following day, Ben headed out to the University Lab mindful to test a new theory. While driving through the morning mist, he spotted two signs on the road:

"They are made with aborted baby fetal cells"

"You can't be Pro-Life and Pro Vax"

Arriving at work. Ben became pensive. Charlie met him in the parking lot getting out of his car.

"Last night something big came to me," Ben's tone was sobering. "Let's find some time to review it off the clock."

Inside the Lab, they tackled some of their usual grant work, to appease their department head. Over the lunch hour, Ben waved a finger at his faithful associate to follow him into the back of the lab. There, he retrieved a flash drive from inside his pocket. Shortly, a three-dimensional projection screen came to life showing a large double-helix DNA strand. Flipping a switch, celtic music flowed down from ceiling speakers to muffle their voices.

"This must be key to the whole thing," Ben spoke in a hush, signaling to Charlie.

"Listen, last night I could not sleep thinking about all of this. Finally, I remembered how in 1953, Dr. Francis Crick and Dr. James Watson were credited with discovering the double helix structure of the human DNA. Later, in an interview, Dr. Crick mentioned finding 144,000 total genes in the human genome. But after Crick and Watson died, scientists reduced this number to the same amount apes have!"

"Wow!" Charlie interjected. "Was it a cover-up to protect the theory of evolution, or something?"

"Exactly!" Ben continued. "We were onto the change of DNA, but I found something that ties everything together. It's physical. It's spiritual." Moving a bright green pointer over the large Double Helix DNA image on the screen, he elaborated; "It's somewhat elementary, and yet so awesome, considering God's incredibly designed genome. Walking under the screen, he raised his arm shining the laser light, "Each double helix strand of DNA has 72,000 genes on either side. One side from the mother and the other from the father. How much does that add up to?"

"144,000."

"Simple, so far, right?" Waving at the screen, another image materialized. "This mRNA adds another strand of DNA to the genome. A third strand here," he pointed out. "Another 72,000."

A moment later, their department chair, Dr. Pidgeon, poked his head into the room by the door. "What's going on in here?" he questioned. Ben quickly switched the screen graphic to show two strands of DNA, instead of three.

"Nothing really," Charlie shrugged. "Were just solving all the problems of the world for you."

"We will be right out for lunch," Ben placated.

After waiting a minute for the smoke to clear, Charlie motioned for Ben to continue. "The physical I get, but why is the third strand so significant, spiritually?"

"Will humans no longer be made in God's image?" Ben asked. He paused considering the gravity of the statement. "Let's do the math. Our creator is the Great mathematician."

Charlie took the laser light, sliding the third DNA strand back up on the screen. He clicked to add a small calculator window below. "So 72 + 72 +72 = 216...It adds up to 216,000.

"Keep in mind the 144,000 is significant in Bible prophecy." Reaching for his cell phone, Ben read from a Bible App:

"Then I looked and behold on Mount Zion stood the Lamb—that's Jesus after his return and victory over the devil—*and with Him the 144,000 who had His name and his Father's names written on their foreheads. They were those who had not taken the Mark of the Beast."* See the devil has a false Mark for mankind, but the Holy Spirit seals the believer with God's true mark..."

"Keep going Ben!"

"So—what's the number of the Mark of the Beast?"

"Everyone knows it's 666..."

"In the original biblical texts, it's really *not* 666. It's a *times* and *half a times* formula. Plainly speaking, it's supposed to be 6 x 60 x 600. Ben signaled for Charlie to do the math on the screen.

"So six, times sixty, times six hundred, is...216,000!"

Charlie reeled, emphasizing the number. There was a *holy hush*, before either one spoke further.

"No wonder you think it could be the *'Mark of the Beast...'*"

"And it's all leading to transhumanism..."

"So what will we do with this information?"

"We plant seeds."

"Seeds?"

You know—we share in a healthy and stealthy way. We plant seeds of information. Like the Cole Report we planted in the hands of discerning doctors and scientists. We use whatever platforms we have to share the truth.

"But this is a little complicated to explain..."

"Just ask: 'If it changes the DNA—could it be the Mark?'"

"That should get their attention."

"Jesus warns that a lot of people will not have 'ears to hear.' In the end we ask, 'why would anyone want to risk their eternal salvation on a man-made shot?'"

"I have to admit, Ben—I don't know anyone in the pharma industry who is a *'Born-Again Believer'* like the Bible says."

That night, Ben discussed the 3rd strand of DNA with Sara. She elaborated, "I wonder how the Lord will respond when people arrive at the *Pearly Gates of Heaven*, with DNA that has been altered. No longer made in the image of God?"

"Will Jesus say *'Away—I never knew you?'*" he venerated.

Switching gears, Ben mentioned his co-worker. "Charlie has really been opening up to me at work. He's a type of Bruce Willis, looks-wise but with a kinder disposition—and a non-drinker, he confided."

Charlie, was a man short in stature, balding, stocky, but fit. He often hit the gym on campus, right after working at the lab each day. "I'm sure some nice lady would like this type of character," Ben mentioned.

"Maybe we need to have him over for dinner to meet Miriam, from next door."

"A blind date?"

"What's a better way for him meet a sweet Christian gal?" Sara's wheels began turning for a favorite dish to prepare.

Over the weekend, thousands were watching Live as Pastor A.J. spoke openly about the mRNA vaccines and their counterparts. At the service, the Prophecy Now message was kept lighter for the first several minutes, ending on a cliffhanger. A.J. stopped abruptly with teaser, "For those wanting to know more, please continue to our church website directly for the rest of the story—the link is on the bottom of your screen."

"They're designed to encode cells with the seed of Satan," he revealed. "The bio weapons may have come from a military base research facility right in North Carolina." He spoke about the cashless society, video surveillance the tracking of humans and explained the *Mark of the Beast* would be required to Buy or Sell, according to the Book of Revelation.

"It's not going to be a chip *'On'* your hands or *'On'* your forehead. The King James Bible says it will be *'In'* your hand or *'In'* your forehead, according to Revelation 13: 16 to 17.

Whenever A.J. mentioned the vaccinations, he referred to them as *Shots, Jabs, Inoculations, Injections, Serums* and a few times even referred to them as the *'Serpents Poison.'*

He often placed large pictures on the screen that coincided with his talks. "Tell me that this long needle doesn't look like a set of fangs. Revelation 15:7 says; *'And one of the four beasts gave unto the seven angels seven golden Vials full of the wrath of God.'* These are the Plagues of the seven angels. Do you know what is held in vials? Aren't serums held in vials? The Bible says we are to *'be as wise as serpents and gentle as doves,'* There is revelation here—are the shots a wrath of God?"

It worked miracles moving the *Prophesy Now* message to the website. Over the next few services there were thousands watching weekly seeking the truth of God. Many people reached out professing that they had accepted Jesus. Others responded online, promising not to take the shots.

They warned family, friends, or co-workers and applied for exemptions at work. Some shared how they had repented for taking the injections.

The following month, A.J. shared, "The Bible states that repentance is turning from the behavior. It leads to a changed life. Lots of preachers say John the Baptist was in the river saying to repent, but the truth is that Jesus preached on repentance too. The Bible says that *after* he was baptized, Jesus *resisted* the devil in the desert. It says resist!"

"Then it says, *'Jesus began his ministry of repentance.'* You won't hear that talked about by these *Prosperity Gospel preachers*!" A sign on the church site read: **"Remember being sorry for something is not the same as repenting of it. Resist!**

After the service, Sara taught a children's class. Ben met with Pastor A.J. to discuss their lab findings on the shots and the 3rd strand of DNA they had discovered.

The Pastor was quick to understand the ramifications;

"Scripture says we are created in His image and our *'Bodies are the temples of the Holy Spirit.'*" A.J. often ran his thick fingers through his long greying beard when contemplating.

"Is this grieving the Holy Spirit then? Is it *'The Abomination'* or *'Mark'*?" They entered into a lengthy discussion on the importance of Ben's findings.

Finally, it was determined that Ben would prepare a synopsis for the Pastor to consider in his online sermons, or to be placed on the website now viewed by thousands each week; Ben contributing the scientific, or physical and A.J. adding to the spiritual implications.

THE FINAL SEED

On the drive home, Sara said, "You know when the Holy Spirit is at work. Every week people are coming to Jesus, from a little country church."

"There was *standing room only* at the church today," Ben added. "We will have to meet outside by the river soon."

"And God is good," she pinched him.

"All the time!" Ben answered her sentence. "And did you see Charlie coming forward at the end of the service? Wow!"

"Hallelujah!" Sara exclaimed. "And Mariam wants to be Baptized as an adult too!"

That night Ben wrote a post for the Church website:

The Genetic scientists that studied the genome for over 25 years came to the conclusion that the human genome—the double helix—had 72,000 genes on each side of the helix. When combined, it totaled 144,000 genes, in the human genome. A genome is the full set of coding or "instructions" made by God, that determine how an organism will develop.

In Revelation 7: 3-4 The Lord references 144,000 as those who have the seal of God. This is a biblical number designating those who belong to the Lord. It's His signature. They're connected in the middle, it's the twisted ladder of the double helix. Man is now trying to alter God's creation. The new mRNA technology given by injection, introduced a third strand of DNA, using a CRISPR splicing technique, inserting it into man's genome, altering DNA. The messaging technology breaks a strand in an edit to the genome, creating a triple helix. The CRISPR sorcery scientists cut up DNA in an organism's genome and edit its sequence. Cell lines used in the vaccines come from replicated aborted baby fetal tissue.

There are 72,000 genes on each need side of the helix, one running down the right side and one running down the left, one strand of the mom, and one strand of the dad, totaling the 144,000, and resulting in the created Holy image of God. When you add another 72,000 genes from the third strand, now you have the triple helix, totaling 216,000. Now everyone choosing to get these injections—that have been given to the entire world, say they are not 'The Mark.'

Many say, 'it is a precursor' and do not warn about what the Bible truly says about this. So, if the number of the beast is 666, or as the Bible States, '600 three score and six.' Then the 600 x 60 x 6, totals to 216,000, or the 'number of his name.' Whos' name? The devils. It is Lucifers name. And there is something in these shots called 'Luciferase.' Pray for God to reveal His truth to you. Pray to stay pure. B. Strickland, PHD

The following day, the Queen of England, of the elitist Windsor family, revealed her allegiance to the NWO and devil's DNA, by lighting up a triple helix on the lawn of Buckingham palace. Watched by much of the world, the ceremony was carried by most every news outlet.

"The Queen just held a pageant mocking God the creator," one of Sara's friends tweeted.

Later in the day, Ben's attorney, Don, called again with breaking news, "Senator Rand is headed back to work and will be reconvening the Senate investigations."

"That's great!" Ben answered.

"It is," But then continuing with the not-so-good-news, his lawyer added, "They've issued a subpoena for you to testify."

"Me? – before the United States Senate?"

"Yes, but Senator Rand is in your corner, Ben. He heard about your talk at the conference. He wants the Cole report."

Chapter 10

"But yet a Tenth will be in it—a Remnant. So the Holy Seed shall be its Stump." Isaiah 6:13.

That night Ben sat up in bed, after another dream rocked him awake. Again, he grabbed the notebook sitting on his nightstand and began writing:

I was driving in a twilight mist through an ancient, yet modern city. Traffic was heavy...

At a forced stop, a tall man in white motions to me. As I exit the car, he beckons me to follow him halting at a large glass door. There he poses a question like a riddle:

"Through this doorway you will find what you asked about and are searching for. It will be something you will come away with, yet hold nothing in your hands."

Intrigued, however puzzled, I entered into what appears to be a Heavenly music store. Gazing upwards to the high glass walls, I noticed giant marble pillars displaying all manner of gold and crystal harps, colorful flutes and the like, which were uniquely crafted, yet unknown to me. Lighting up in wonder, I heard a deep voice behind me:

"Are you here to investigate?" an older shopkeeper pointed up, from behind the counter.

"Would it be possible to play an instrument?" I replied.

"Yes," he smiled. "However, the real answer you seek has to do with the prayer you seeded."

Standing next to this man stood a white-haired woman, who calmly said, "The answer to your question is: 'Yes,'"...

Instinctively, I remembered before falling asleep, I had said a short prayer: "Dear Lord, show me if what we're witnessing right now, unfolding through these shots, is truly 'The Mark.'"

The man nodded at me, as if to say: "You understand then." Smiling to put me at ease, he said the word: ***"Yes."*** Then sullenly, he confirmed: "It seals Unholy Mark."

Feeling light-headed, I nodded in acknowledgment and walked quickly outside. The tall man wearing white remained by the entrance. Without his speaking, I heard audible words:

"You have your answer then—now awaken."

The moonlight glow shone through the curtains. Ben closed his notebook, considering the dream, closing his eyes, hoping to recall more details. Then saying a silent prayer to Him who gives generously, for all of those who ask.

A moment later, Sara stirred at his side, "You awake sweetie?"

Sharing the dream with Sara, she was filled with awe. "Before falling asleep I read, Matthew 13, It's all about the Seeds!" Finding the page in her Bible, she read:

Another parable Jesus put forth unto them, saying,

"The kingdom of heaven is likened unto a man which sowed good seed in his field: But while men slept, his enemy came and sowed tares among the wheat, and went his way. Let both grow together until the harvest: and in the time of harvest, I will say to the reapers, Gather ye together first the tares, and bind them in bundles to burn them: but gather the wheat into my barn." And his disciples came unto him, saying, "Declare unto us the 'meaning of' the parable of the tares of the field."

"Jesus answered and said unto them, 'He that soweth the good seed is the Son of man; The field is the world; the good seed are the children of the kingdom; but the tares are the children of the wicked one; The enemy that sowed them is the devil; the harvest is the end of the world; and the reapers are the angels. As therefore the tares are gathered and burned in the fire; so shall it be in the end of this world."

Nestling under the covers, she contemplated, "Spiritually, three groups of people emerge in the end times," Sara reached inside the big book for her notes; "*First*, there are *the Remnants* refusing the devil's mark and its eternal consequences. They're the ones doing the will of God. They're the ones warning others as *Watchmen on the wall,* according to Ezekiel 3 and 33. It says we will be held accountable when we fail to warn others. *That the blood will be on our hands.*" Sara held a small flashlight over the words.

"These are the ones *not* taking the shots," she paused turning a page.

"And they're the ones keeping their bloodlines pure," Ben agreed.

"Secondly—there are those who took the injections. Possibly the only way out is to repent, for trusting in man and medicine over God. They followed the devil's plan. They trusted the world over the Lord for protection and provision. Some were driven by fear. Others were often coerced by friends, family or work to take the injection. Many are pushing to inject the children. I'm just sick about it—all my innocent preschoolers!"

"And the Bible says, *'and they did not repent of their Sorceries,'* Ben added, "and the translation of '*Sorcery,*' is '*Pharmakeia;*' *drugs, medicine, poison* and even *witchcraft.*"

"What's the third category? Ben asked.

"They're the ones who may not be saved yet. But for some reason they did not take the shots. Maybe it's for health or personal reasons. Maybe they don't trust authority."

"Maybe they're just smart!" Ben reached over to turn out the light. "Hopefully, this group has a better chance of turning to Jesus later on." In the stillness, they let the quiet of night breathe over them for a time.

A muffled cry broke from her side of the bed. "I'm sorry that we have no children, Ben."

"Maybe it's me," he responded, clutching her hand under the covers. "You never know hon, remember God blessed Abraham and Sara with a child. Wasn't she 90 years old or something?" He waited, hearing her stifle a few more tears.

Trying to lighten the situation, he followed with, "At ninety years old—no wonder Sara in the Bible had such a hard time believing she was pregnant."

Sara hesitated before answering. "It is a comforting thought." Moving closer she sniffled, "But I'm older now."

"Hey, you're only the halfway mark to the hundred-dollar bill and you look like a twenty."

As they dozed off, Ben prayed for his wife. Earlier, he had explained the spiritual importance of the third strand of DNA to her. She had immediately digested the concept of 216,000. The third strand as the mark concept.

The following day, Ben contemplated their midnight talk.

There's another group of people concerning the injections and their spiritual ramifications.

Handing Sara a blended fruit smoothy, he said, "Have you noticed the ones not taking the shots are more open to salvation? This group of people refusing the shots, are not so fear based. Maybe they're more rebellious, or spiritually minded to false ideas. They may still turn to Jesus."

"The Bible says without turning to the cross, by the blood of Jesus for our sins, there is no hope," she answered. "We've warned so many people who are blindly taking them—many saying they're Christians—are we missing something here?"

Ben led them in the short prayer, "Lord we pray for Your grace to reveal further truth here and *Show us Everything…*"

"Help us to reach the ones resisting the shots open to faith," she pleaded. "Help them to receive *Your Mark. Your Seal!*"

Opening their Bible to Ephesians 1:3, provided a hopeful answer, *'When you **believed**, you were **Marked** in Him with a **Seal**, the promised Holy Spirit.'* "They need faith!" Ben said.

The ride to work was slower than usual. Many were back on the road with a *business as usual*, attitude; *The New Normal.*

A call from his nephew soon blared over the car speakers.

"I'm quitting work Uncle Ben—my boss is a genocidal maniac."

Ben choose his words carefully, "His father was an attorney for Planned Parenthood—no excuse though," he clarified.

"I read his mother had worked for IBM, back in the day. The division responsible for doing the first tracking cards on the Jews in World War II." *The 'Apple doesn't fall very far from the tree,'* Ben thought.

"Check your encrypted messages Uncle Ben, there's a video you need to see. It's a little *'freaky'.* Its about *faith'*—got to go,"—the line went dead.

Later, on the drive home from the lab, the days further genome discoveries weighed heavily. Third strand *crisper technology* morphed into more practical innovations, *the button to my garage door opener would make me a sorcerer to my great-grandparents. Would it be another restless night in bed?*

Ben postponed watching the video, sent by his nephew,

realizing the enemy would try and invade his thoughts and dreams when such demonstrative things were ingested before sleep. It was almost noon the next day, before Ben recalled his nephew's words, *the video is a little freaky about faith…*the video from over a decade before.

In the video, what appears to be a younger version of William Bates, is briefing Bureau agents about a project titled '*FUNVAC*', about the human VMAP2 gene, also known as '*The God gene*' that can be altered using a vaccine.

Billy whined on, "So, our hypothesis here is that there are fanatical people that have an over expression of the gene. By vaccinating them against this with a type of serum, we will eliminate this fanatic religious behavior," he tells the government agents. Directing their attention to a large screen, he continues, "On the left over here we have those individuals who are religious fundamentalists, religious fanatics, they express the VMAP2 gene, on the right we have a normal person who shows disgust when presented with reading from a religious text."

Shockingly, one agent in the briefing mentions spreading a virus, "to contain independent thought processes in individuals." Then another agent responds, "So are you suggesting I run a CT scan to evaluate people to determine whether I need to put a bullet in their head?"

Then pointing to the large screen, Bates explains no need to do a CT scan, "Because the virus we give will immunize the VMAP2 Gene, and that would have the effect you see here, which would essentially stop these religious fanatics."

The bureau agent responds, "So how do you propose this would be dispersed—via spraying?"

Bates responds, "So the present plan and tests we have done so far, uses the *FUNVAC*, to give respiratory viruses, such as the flu, or coronaviruses. We believe this is the best way for exposure to the largest population. We're confident this will be a very successful approach," he ends.

Ben sat stunned for a minute, after watching the old video. *They've been telling us all along.* He remembered reading in the Cole report about the Military testing these types of aerosols over San Francisco many years before in the 60's.

THE FINAL SEED

Even now they're spraying the skies; the white clouds being formed in most areas, contained aluminum, strontium and barium, he had discovered. All three metals would poison the earth, be absorbed in lungs and work with the 5G.

And now with the whammy of the toxic nano-injections, he realized the goal was for the hive mind.

To destroy faith and the seed of man has been the enemy's goal since the Garden of Eden.

After explaining the details of the video to Sara, he elaborated, "Marshal is finally ready to quit working for Bates after twenty years—think this was the nail in the coffin for him."

"What do you think the video really means, Ben?

"If it plays out, it means they have been plotting this for years. It's a multi-pronged approach. They evidently broadened their original plan. It's designed to kill people's individual will—designed to kill people's faith in God."

"If it's ever released online, they will probably just call it a fake," she lamented. "But there's always hope." Sara touched his shoulder, "We're *Born Again* not of *Corruptible Seed*, but *Incorruptible*, it says in the Word of God."

"Yes—the seed that falls on the good soil, and thrives." Then switching into research doctor mode, Ben analyzed, "The right middle front of the gyrus is the part of the brain associated with intents, beliefs, desires—associated with the theories of individual will and the mind."

"The Soul," she nods.

"Since this briefing by Bates, years ago, it has spiraled out of control from using these toxins against the religious fanatics in the Middle East to Christians and the entire planet. They're not only searing the pineal gland, or killing off a faith gene, but are corrupting the DNA, the Holy Seed of man; a plan of the devil all along."

At church that week, Pastor A.J. was excited with Ben and Sara's idea to provide faith-based exemption letters online, to people fighting to stay un-jabbed. During the message, now viewed weekly by thousands, an online banner read: "*With your email request, we will send you an Exemption Form to use for work, so you don't have to take any DNA altering abominations.*

Departing from his recent series, preaching on Revelation, A.J. opened, "We're going to be living in the books of Acts here today."

Sharing the story of Pentecost with Peter and John on the steps of the Temple, he went on, "The people who denied Christ asked, *'What shall we do to be saved then?'* In Acts 2:38 Peter responded, *'Repent and be baptized all of you, in the name of Jesus Christ, for the remission of sin and you shall receive the gift of the Holy Spirit.'*

So today, after the service, we're heading out to the little river behind *The Little White Church* for some baptisms! We encourage you Holy Spirit filled believers everywhere to baptize others by full immersion in water, with repentance in the name of Jesus, for the forgiveness of sins. I pray now for the *gift of the Holy Spirit to fall upon you*!"

Ben and Sara looked at each other "I've only been baptized as a baby," she whispered.

"Same with me," Ben responded innocently.

"Come on," she lit up. "Let's get baptized for real today right in the river!"

"In our clothes?"

"Sure..."

"Well, I don't think the Pastor would take kindly to me in my boxers," he winked.

Signs of summer were all around them, as the rocks beside the brook felt warm to the feet. There was a bubbling falls on the other side of the flowing stream they called *The River*.

One small boy, around the age of ten, suddenly jumped from the top of a rock down into the pool of deeper water.

Landing with perfect precision, he began swimming in their direction.

Standing by Ben and Sara, the boys' mother commented how her son had been coming to the swimming hole for many years. "Daniel," she called, "are you going to be getting baptized today?"

The young boy looked up at Ben and Sara, from the brisk stream, "This will be my fourth time," he said excitedly. "Everybody is so afraid now—but I'd rather die for Jesus, than to die of old age!"

When it came time for Ben and Sara's turn to be baptized, Pastor A.J. leaned each one of them back, one at a time into the water, first asking: "Do you repent of your sin and profess Jesus Christ of Nazareth, as your Lord and Savior?

"I do," each answered.

"It won't be an easy path," A.J. paused, with hands supporting each of their backs in the cool water, "but I think you already know that."

"Yes, but Jesus will be with us," Sara said.

"And He will guide us through every storm," Ben finished.

On the drive through the thick carpet of green trees home, Ben kept hearing the words from the baptism, *'It won't be easy'...*

Sara was surprised to find their new Akita sleeping soundly. In recent days, the large dog was found waiting by the front door, when they returned home.

"She's not sleeping!" Sara reacted with alarm. Bending down, she checked the dog's pulse, lifting an eyelid simultaneously. "She's been drugged, Ben!"

Cautiously, he searched around the home, opening the doors to each room slowly, as Sara worked to revive the dog.

Finally, Sara heard a loud, "Great! just great..." she knew her husband all too well, even more so now after all of the time spent together during the lockdowns. She *knew the reaction signaled annoyance.*

Running to the back of their home, Ben was standing in the middle of the office.

"Similar to our workplace after the break-in," he grumbled, "but this feels much more personal."

"Anything missing?"

"Still checking," he rifled through the drawers and cabinets. "Would have added those security cameras, but the pros will just disconnect them," the corners of his mouth turned downward. Searching around the room he held up their marriage certificate. "Well, you can't have this!" he resounded. Ben held up one finger motioning them outside.

"How's the dog?"

"Thank God, Kimmy is reviving."

Outside he quietly whispered, "It sounds like a bad film, but they might have placed a bug in our home somewhere."

"And to threaten us, maybe," she nodded, reaching into her purse still drooped around her neck. 'They don't realize we will not go quietly, because we have this!" Clasping onto her Bible, she held it high. Reaching down, the Kita was nudging her leg in comfort. "Oh Kimmy! she cried, hugging her huge pup.

Ben shook his head, "Our attack dog's name is Kimmy..."

Later, he reported to the Deputy Sheriff that nothing much was taken, "A couple financial files are missing," he offered.

"Well, you better cancel your credit cards," the Sheriff advised.

Ben had not wanted to share the lengthy details of their journeys with the clandestine medical report, by Dr. Cole, the conference, or recent break-ins at work.

"We would truly appreciate you driving by our home and neighborhood daily for a while," Ben requested, as the Deputy was departing.

"Absolutely," came the resolute response, "absolutely."

After dinner, their neighbor, Miriam, stopped by to receive instructions on taking care of the dog and their home, while they were away in D.C.

"You had the Sheriff here?" Miriam wondered.

"A personal matter," Sara offered, explaining how the poor dog got caught up in their cross-fire and that Ben would be testifying before the Senate in a couple of days.

"Last week there were two men by your car in the driveway and Kimmy chased them away. I meant to tell you. From my porch I had a nice vantage point." Miriam kneeled down to pet the big dog, still somewhat groggy. "Good girl, good girl."

"Did you get a look at them?" Ben inquired.

"Not really. It was late. I noticed they were dressed in suits. Too nice for census takers or contact tracers," Miriam finished.

The following morning before work, Ben met Charlie in the lobby, "Our home invasion was much like the break-in we had last year here. We need to be more careful what we say inside these ivory walls. My gut tells me it was the same ones. Maybe they make a mess to distract and plant a bug for eavesdropping."

"They could be after our medical research too," Charlie weighed in. "They would know by now there are other copies of the Cole report."

"And they are tracking who we gave them to?"

"Exactly."

Ben held up a small flash drive retrieved from a front pants pocket. "This has everything we have ever discovered. Never leaves my side."

"Do you sleep with it under your pillow, too?"

Upstairs in the lab, an assistant handed him a memo. It was from their department head, Dr. Pidgeon:

"It has come to my attention that you are under a United States Senate inquiry. Any information to be shared must be cleared through this office. All genetic research, papers and discovery, since your employment, must be submitted for my review by the end of this week." Dr. H. Gerald Pidgeon

Catching a glance of the memo, Charlie smirked, "Makes you wonder how *The Pidgeon* comes by such information."

Chapter 11

"They tracked our steps, so we could not walk in our streets—the occupying troops harassed [the remnant] at every opportunity."
Lamentations 4:18

It would be more than a six-hour drive to Washington D.C., for the Senate hearing. Ben took some comfort in the words from his lawyer, "Senator Rand is on your side, Ben."

For security, they were advised not to lodge at the Capitol. Leaving a day early, Ben wanted to break up the drive, "Your desire to visit Colonial Williamsburg in Virginia is finally coming true," he surprised her.

It dawned on Sara, during the drive, there was so much vast expanse still left in the country. *Powers that be pushing people into cloistered areas with concrete and 5G.* "'Smart Cities,' sound like a 'dumb idea'," she laughed unexpectedly.

Sara knew that listening to praise songs on the drive, would *take our minds out of this worldly D'A'Z'E*—she sounded each letter to herself. Singing was a wonderful way to overcome these demands, free from subpoenas, politics or shots. Hadn't her grandma often said, "One hundred years from now, what difference will it all make?" *What a blessing driving through such magnificent surroundings in the country,* she delighted.

Joyfully, they burst out singing on many favorite old hymns. *What a wonderful way to overcome the anxiety about what is coming at the Capitol.*

"What's the real purpose of a Senate hearing?" she asked.

Turning down the volume, Ben responded, "Our attorney from the conference went on at length preparing me for the format. They hold hearings in order to gather information; review discrepancies, including corporations and even their own rogue government agencies. They investigate possible wrongdoings." The fall leaves were glowing in color, making their descent on the Blue Ridge Highway even more breathtaking. Quietly, they sat for a time, contemplating the splendor.

"I've been praying for Senator Rand and his family," Sara broke the silence. "All the rest of Congress are bought off."

"He convened the committee right after getting out of the hospital," Ben mentioned. "I hope they not only investigate, but prosecute the wrongdoings and medical tyranny by the pharmaceuticals."

"They're supposed to be protecting people," Sara added. "Congressmen taking money need to be prosecuted too."

Ben drove on incessantly, "Rand's pursuing criminal investigations of the U.S. infectious disease, head Dr. Fausti. He needs to resign. The NIH was involved with the origin of the Covid pandemic and patented viruses, and protocols used to supposedly combat what they created..."

Finally arriving in Colonial Williamsburg, Sara gushed, "This is like walking around in a living history museum!" Sara was in her element strolling historic Main Street, littered with bright colored shops with local artists. The Capitol building, and Governor's Palace appeared in the distance, transporting them into the 18th century. Historic residences lined the side streets. Some were open for viewing.

"Imagine living in an era like this," she said. "No cell phones, 5G, chemtrails or pharma."

Ben interjected, "No electricity though."

"Sign me up anyway," she beamed.

"Maybe we need to find a candle shop."

Ducking around the corner, by the Merchants Market, a sign over the store read, *Back in the Day*. Behind the counter was an older woman wearing granny glasses. Noticing Ben, donning a 3-point hat reminiscent of the Revolutionary War, she commented, "You would make an excellent Paul Revere."

He replied, "a shoemaker by trade, right?"

"Repaired them mostly," the gray-haired gal wore a high collar dress with ruffles around the neck. "Paul Revere also struck his own coins," she added. "In those days, 95% of the country was owned by small business. A different time." Then seemingly out of nowhere, she pointed to a case filled with old coins. "With what is coming—I'd buy some coins."

"Old coins?" Sara was intrigued. "Why?"

"Old or new, it doesn't really matter. Just make it silver or gold just like your grandpa. They always put some food stores down too. Great grandma would have had a cellar under the home, chocked full."

Then looking around the room she lowered her voice, "Listen, you seem like a nice couple," she said. "It's about all these things happening now, like the injections they want us all to take. Or the cashless society coming—you know if you don't take them, you won't be able to *Buy or Sell*."

"We're with you on this one," Sara nodded. Reaching into her purse, Sara retrieved one of the tiny Little Bibles they often shared. "It has one verse from each book in the Bible."

"Well, I have a big one from the 1600's. Its my bedtime comfort almost every night," she laughed.

"Those who think like us are hard to find. Rare. We need to build support for each other," Ben finished. Poking around in the back of the shop, he was elated to find *The Scientific Journal* of *Natural Healing Remedies*, 1887. Sara took the time to engage the shop owner further, exchanging contact information.

"Sally said we can leave the SUV parked in front of her store. She lives upstairs."

"Who's Sally?

Grabbing Ben's hand, Sara led him outside pointing up at the sign, "She owns *Back in the Day*—I really like her. They've had some break-ins at the Bed and Breakfast parking lot."

"And she has security cameras," he noticed gazing up.

E ntering their room, at the Inn, Ben read from yellowed newspaper article framed atop the mantle of a brick fireplace.

"This says Charlton Heston, the actor, stayed right in this very room over an entire summer, when he was younger. He was a manager at the local playhouse over 50 years ago."

Reclining on a fluffy pillow, Sara mused, "Think of it— Moses slept in this canopy bed."

"Hoping the mattress is newer than that," he chuckled.

Before falling asleep, she nestled deep into his chest. The box springs rattled with the smallest movement. "Maybe we need to start warning more people about what's coming," she whispered—and like the lady in the shop said, 'buy some coins and store some food.'"

"Organic foods are fast disappearing." Ben rattled the bed with concern, "Scripture says we will held accountable for not warning others."

"Well, you will be warning the Senate tomorrow," she held him tightly. "Maybe with the world watching on TV too. I'm proud of you, Ben."

He thought of responding with another verse, *'Pride cometh before the fall,'* but instead, relished this time in her arms. *That phone on the nightstand will ring all too soon, with a morning wake up call. Better get some shut eye before testifying.*

Bright and early, Ben played a thoughtful message from the evening before. Pastor A.J. encouraged, "We're all praying for you both—for your protection, safe travels and truth to be revealed." It went on for a while with the Pastor closing in a prayer, Ben's head shot up from the sink while he was shaving, ***"May no weapon formed against you prosper!"***

Did prophetic A.J. know they would be needing protection?

Checking the time, Ben switched into high gear. "I'll load the SUV and be right back with the car," he told Sara.

Grabbing both of their bags, he made large strides towards the vehicle parked by old Sally's shop.

Abruptly, his cell phone rang. Pausing to answer, the screen read: *Private.* On any given day, these calls went unanswered, yet now with the Senate testimony looming in a few hours; "Yes?" he answered.

"Ben?—Ben Strickland?" Without waiting for a response, the voice marched on. "Where are you, Ben? Are you alone? Is your wife with you? Thank God you answered. Listen—you are both in grave danger."

"Who is this?" *It sounded like Dr. Cole...*

"So sorry—yes, Cole. Right now, men are coming for you. Its usually two—they use tracers."

In a moment, Ben started to jog down Main Street. Spotting the SUV, jarred a memory, *The Cole Report and my Testimony are hidden inside the trunk.* Dropping the bags, he began sprinting towards the vehicle. Scanning the street while running, he focused on a parked black van. *Could that be two men inside?*

Ducking behind his own SUV, Ben opened the hatch quickly retrieving the files hidden under the well, by the spare tire. Immediately, from across the street, the doors of the black van flung open. Two men in dark suits were moving rapidly in his direction. One had a shock of familiar blond hair. *They spotted me*, Ben knew.

Without time to close the hatch door, Ben retreated down the sidewalk. The two men gained on him, crossing his way. Reaching the intersection, two horse drawn carriages momentarily blocked the advancing men in suits.

A moment later, a bright rose-colored pickup truck pulled up, alongside Ben. "Hop in!" hollered a grey-haired lady from behind the wheel. It was Sally from the shop. Sara was inside the truck. Scooting to the middle of the front-seat, she helped pull Ben inside.

"Helps to have a few friends," Sally revved the engine, waving at the men driving the two carriages. "Hold on—My F150 has a Hemi under the hood!"

Dashing down a side-street in the big pickup, Ben looked back to see the two men in suits, already getting behind the wheel of the van for pursuit; clutching tightly to the reports in his hands brought a comfort of sorts.

"We'll see if I can lose them," Sally was charged up. "They don't know these back roads like I do..." the big tires squealed.

"Last night, the cameras picked up those guys checking out your car. Then when I saw that black van this morning,.."

"So glad you found me at the Inn," Sara closed her eyes as the truck hit a jarring bump. The van was a speck now.

Reaching for his cell phone, Ben phoned their attorney in Washington, filling him in on the call from Dr. Cole, their whereabouts and current harrowing predicament of pursuit.

"Hold the phone a minute," the lawyer hesitated, adding, "Don't hang up!" He came back on the line in blazing speed, "Head right to the private Williamsburg Airport. The back gate will be open. Look for a helicopter with the rotors turning." The lawyer added, "And call me when you are in the air!"

"I know right where that is," Sally hugged the wheel tightly;

"We're not far." Several minutes flashed by; F150 horsepower gunning along the narrow two-lane straightaway. Now the along the back road, a tall chain-link fence appeared; then on the other side, several small Cessna's and a Piper Cub.

"Over there!" Sara snapped to attention. "Those helicopter blades are turning!"

Sally slowed the truck as they scanned along the fence for an open gate. Now the black van in pursuit began gaining ground. Turning a hard right through a small opening in the fence, the rear of the truck slid sideways. Correcting the wheel in the opposite direction, brought it under control. The black van slid past in a blur.

"They will have to turn around now!" Sally laughed. "No time for goodbyes," she hit the brakes hard, spinning the truck around close to the whirring blades.

Tugging at Sara's hand out of the pickup, it felt like walking into a sandstorm towards the small portal door of the copter;

clothing fought violently against their bodies as the wind from the rotors blew overhead.

Inside, the pilots' headset was buzzing along with the blades above. Without a prompt, each buckled a seatbelt. As the black van pulled up alongside Sally's truck, the small helicopter began its rapid ascent angled forward. Ben noticed coffee stains on the worn carpet. Splotches of rusted metal hinted at the crafts age. The throttle resembled a motor-cycle twist grip mounted on the control.

Finally, the pilot spoke, "They gave us a special clearance—

We will be at the Capitol in a buster—I'm retired Military," he tried reassuring, "So nothing to worry about."

Sara gave a knowing smile to her husband.

He's Military—what is the definition of irony, Ben stifled a laugh, as their bodies shuddered aloft.

Saying a silent prayer helped him regain composure. One scripture came to mind that surprisingly gave comfort: *"Whoever shall save his life, shall lose it, but whoever shall lose his life for my sake and Gospel's, the same shall save it..."*

In minutes he would be testifying before the Senate. Over the Potomac River, Sara squeezed Ben's hand tightly. Shortly, the Washington Monument came into view, opening to the Capitol Mall, the MLK, Lincoln and Jefferson memorials. Ben bristled as they circled over the George Washington Masonic Temple. *God, prepare me for the battle of today,* Ben prayed, *Your words not mine...*

The pilot handled the descent at the Capitol with skill, feathering upwards at the last moment, before touching down. A white Capitol transport drove them the short distance to the Senate. Immediately, they were ushered in through security, scanned and given wristbands. Lanyards with each of their names were placed around their necks.

Within a half hour, Senator Rand had introduced Ben saying, "Dr. Strickland has seven minutes for his opening statement—please proceed, if you will."

Dr. Benjamin Stricklands Statement before the Senate:

"These injections with mRNA are not medicine," Ben began.

"These are gene altering technologies with an intra-body Nano Network, presently administered through the injections. Nano patches are now undergoing mock trials.

The shots have likely killed millions of people already.

THE FINAL SEED

"Pathologists and medical researchers are finding these are not blood clots, as revealed by post mortem autopsies; They are self-assembling self-replicating nanotechnology, lipid nanoparticles that have been modified on a molecular level wrapped in pegulation; polyethylene glycol. It's Graphene Oxide—one of the components used to make hydrogel.

"The lipid nanoparticles are modified to be sensitive to heat infrequency. When placed in the human body, they become energized by the heat. With that excitement, Nanofection created in the particles slowly drifts towards each other. Hence, they become self-assembling. This intra-body Nano network is the first step to make the human body a device linked into the internet of bodies. A physical hive controlled by AI—Artificial Intelligence, now in place. An injected person emits EMF. Anyone can check this with a Bluetooth AP in developer mode.

"The shots also change DNA, rendering the person a GMO owned by a corporation, according to the patents. This allows the system to harvest psychological, biological, genetic and physiological data from an individual without their knowledge or consent. People technically become products owned by the corporation who holds the patents of the given injections," He paused letting the gravity of it all sink in—Ben's voice had been filled with a steady stream of *heaping coals*.

"Hold on there," one Senator interrupted, but with the wave of a hand, Rand silenced him. "Please continue Dr. Strickland."

"Have any of you studied one of these toxic vials under an electron microscope?" he asked rhetorically. "I have...

The Pentagon refers to these as *Counter Measures*. Isn't that a term used for weapons? It was DARPA, with forty-eight billion in government contracts. Global corporations such as, Black Rock and Vanguard are involved. The globalists control the monetary and banking systems, with families in Europe; the Rothchilds, Warburgs, Lazards, Seifs, in the States its Goldman Sachs, Rockefellers, Lehmans and Loebs.

"Information—block chain—is the new gold standard, and the foundation for the coming financial system; The CBDC, Central Bank Digital Currency. The Next Step is a quantum dot tattoo that will slowly release quantum microdots, chips into the human body, individualizing and authenticating all data for each individual.

"This is part of a transhuman agenda being initiated on the population without their knowledge by these global elites, working primarily through the WEF, the World Economic Forum, The WHO, the IMF and other global control systems that are not any part of one government. They own governments through manipulation of elections and the financial systems. They control 'AI' and the largest corporations."

Ben peered up cautiously from his prepared text and then improvised. "Does anyone here really get this? Does Congress even hold any power now? No. You gave it away!"

Ben's blood began pumping. "The C.U.R.E. Act and other Legislation gave the power to the Department of Health and Human Services. The head of HHS holds the power. Does anyone know who really controls it? You gave them the power to declare a Health Emergency anytime without oversight. Does this not destroy our Constitution of individual rights?"

Ben picked up the notes again, "In the Jackson vs Pfizer court case, the Pharma Industry was exonerated claiming, and I quote, 'In a joint project, the DOD, Department of Defense, paid Six Billion Dollars for *prototypes*—not *vaccines*. A prototype is for a test, no approval is needed. Therefore, no studies or CDC, FDA approval is necessary.' By Congress giving away its authority, you allowed them to experiment with a deadly concoction on the whole world."

"Hold on there, man," the portly Senator interrupted again.

Undaunted, Ben plowed through his notes, "One man at the HHS has the power to call for quarantines, isolations, forced inoculations, or condemning of property—*taking people out of their homes*," he emphasized. "*Asymptomatic carriers, pre-communicable individuals*, these are *NOT* scientific terms. They pull these terms out of thin air, and apply them to healthy persons, all for their own agenda. Healthy humans are re-classified as Bio-Hazards. Unelected officials are *CALLING ALL THE SHOTS*. No pun intended."

"The HHS dictates the mandates and then contracts with the Defense Department for Bio-Weapons for use on the public. With *ZERO INTERVENTION FROM CONGRESS,* and using *YOUR* funding. When the C.U.R.E. Act was passed, there were three Pharmaceutical Lobbyists for every one member of Congress. How many are there now?"

"STOP!" A Congresswomen riled up, "We can find you in contempt!" Rand held a stifling hand up in her direction.

Ben's attorney nodded for him to continue, "An unelected official at HHS, without oversight or repercussions. Total immunity, like the drug companies—isn't this a health dictatorship?

"Is the plan for this technology to link every human being into the internet of bodies? The foundation for a global CBDC that will be controlled with Quantum systems is here. This technology has the capacity to fully surveil and control every individual," Ben paused. The only audible sound was the humming of a heating and air unit.

"Listen," Ben raised up, "If you haven't figured this out yet, we are in a fight for humanity itself!" Easing back into his seat, he sighed, "There is also a spiritual element for those so inclined—it's in the Report," he held it up for all to see. "There are eternal consequences." Ben's attorney quickly made a motion to Senator Rand for the report to be submitted to the committee.

"Thank you, Dr. Strickland," the curly haired Senator nodded. "Your report will be reviewed and submitted into evidence." Surprisingly, Senator Rand adjourned the committee before any questions could be asked of Ben.

"He's on your side," Ben's lawyer reminded in the foyer, "Rand didn't want any of those cronies digging at you today. He's after the truth."

"Is there anyone who recognizes the gravity in all this?"

"For my money, everything you said in there is true," the attorney patted his shoulder. "At least you got it on record."

Walking the long Congressional corridor back to their waiting van seemed endless. "Humans will become obsolete, the way we are going."

Just when Ben believed all of the drama was over, a man came running in his direction down the stark hallway. The stocky attorney moved quickly to shield Ben. The tension dissipated after seeing Sara trailing behind the running man.

"Uncle Ben!" the man called.

Ben gave a nervous laugh to his lawyer, "It's my nephew."

"Had to see this for myself." A bulky Marshal, leaned over, holding Ben in a tight bear hug. "We're driving you home," he stated matter of factly.

Sara caught up to them, encircling her arms around Ben's neck, giving a big kiss. "You were very courageous in there today, sweetheart."

"We're all staying at the Ambassador," Marshal stated. "My treat—Jessica is already there."

That evening, after dinner Marshal took Ben aside, as the ladies talked. "There's something else, Uncle Ben." Reaching in a briefcase he pulled out a notepad. "It's an internal document. They had a plan to intercept you en-route, or here in Washington. I called in a long overdue favor at work and they were told to backoff."

Ben considered the document with their statistics, and ledger showing the information tracking their steps. It listed a government code at the bottom, including the Senate roster, date and his scheduled time before the committee.

"There are no favors I want from *Mr. Bates*," Ben answered resolutely.

"It was not from Mr. Bates," Marshal replied. "It was from *Mrs. Bates*—His wife, Yolinda. She's divorcing him. Said she's had enough—that he was hanging around with Epstein on his child-trafficking Island."

Chapter 12

"And every one that hath forsaken houses, or brethren, or sisters, or father, or mother, or wife, or children, or lands, for my name's sake, shall receive a hundredfold, and shall inherit everlasting life," Matthew 19:29.

B ack home in the Carolina Mountains, Ben and Marshal compared notes and worked on ways to inform more of the faithful with *'Ears to Hear,'* as Pastor A.J. had encouraged.

Sara enjoyed cooking with Marshal's wife, Jessica, who also had a green thumb.

"Let's plant a garden like this when we get home!" Jessica called to Marshal from the tall tomato vines, one morning. "I'm picking out our dinner."

At the men's Bible breakfast that morning, Ben was asked to share his Senate testimony. Afterward, the group discussed the *War on Remnant Christians,* worldwide. And then persisted with their end-times study.

Wrapping things up, Pastor A.J. posed a question to them: "What is the largest cult in the world?" The men took turns answering one at a time, coming up with religious names such as: *'The Mormons, Scientology, Jehovah Witnesses, the Muslims...'*

"It must be the Pope and the Catholics!" Marshal asserted.

"They have made so-called, 'Climate Change,' a religion, haven't they?" A.J.'s son, James, asked.

A.J. studied the men's faces carefully. "This is something between us," Pastor A.J. lowered his tone most seriously.

"I believe the biggest Cult in the world now—consists of all those people who have taken the DNA altering shots..."

In the parking lot, young James caught up to Ben, "Dr. Strickland, sorry to bother you. But I have a serious question."

"What is it, James?" *Ben was surprised by Pastor A.J.'s son choking back tears.* Clutching his hands, he was soft spoken.

"My girlfriend is pressuring me to get married, but she's had the Moderna and a booster. Will this affect my own health or having kids? So far, I've held out..."

"Ahh, well, that's good James. Research has shown the spike proteins in other people's blood may transfer through the bodily fluids—I'd pray about it and consult the scriptures. I once heard your own dad say, *'What does light have to do with darkness'* and *'do not partake in her abominations...'*"

"I know the Bible says to be *'equally yoked,'*" James nodded.

On the winding drive climbing the hill back home, Marshal asked, "Are all those guys at the men's group shot free?"

"Amazing—isn't it?" Ben replied. "You had a part in that, Marshal," he smiled as his eyes moistened. "And the word of God is powerful and effective." Ben's wet eyes directed their attention to a verse Sara had posted on the dashboard:

*"And for by thy **Pharmakeia**' Sorceries, Drugs, Medicine, were **all** nations deceived."* Rev. 18:23

Arriving home from the men's meeting, they spotted the ladies out front, watering. Sara called out, "Miriam, is here. I asked her to join us for dinner." Sprinting to the SUV, she opened Ben's car door, whispering, "Why don't you see if Charlie is free tonight..."

Later, after a delicious homegrown meal, they bundled up by the outdoor firepit. As the sky loomed darker, Marshal bent over from his big frame, "Almost forgot to mention, when we were coming through security at the airport, my bag got hung up on the belt. Leaning over to retrieve it, there was someone from Homeland Security watching a monitor. They were scanning *people*, Uncle Ben. Not luggage—but people..."

Charlie standing nearby Miriam, perked up his ears, "Did you see what the scanning showed?"

"It looked as if some of those coming through the line had parts of their bodies lighting up on the screen. The bio luminescence appeared to be glowing down their shoulder into the hand. On others it was centered in their foreheads."

"Wow," was all Ben mustered, his eyes fixed on the firepit.

"And on some of them—it was lighting up in both places..."

Their brief time home, had given respite and distraction from the harried world. Ben used his vacation days from the Lab and Sara had a friend covering her shifts at Pre-School. Ignoring cell phones and messages, Ben was unaware several major news media outlets were clamoring for an interview with him.

Word had traveled fast, following Ben's Senate testimony, that a leaked Government report provided details linking the Pentagon directly with pharmaceutical companies. Billions in taxpayer *hush-fund*s were paid covertly to companies like Pfizer and Moderna for the SARS Cov-19 mRNA injectables.

In the case of the start-up, Moderna, they had never even developed an aspirin before.

Covering for Ben at the Lab, Charlie weighed in: "The name really stands for MODeRNA, or 'Modify with mRNA.'" He was a man on a mission now. "Check your memos and messages, Ben—the University is telling us to cease from all work regarding the injectables..."

Drudgingly, Ben listened to the vitriolic messages from his own Department head, Dr. H. Gerald Pidgeon. It was true. There were several caustic calls and emails to cease and desist from researching all pharmaceuticals, viruses. He had finished one call: "Shutdown all communication with the outside world!" At this broad command, Ben found himself musing over the pomp and impossibility. *The 'Writings on the Wall,' for me at work.*

Then, after hearing from his D.C. Lawyer, it became apparent the switchboards were lighting-up from reporters nationwide. All wanted to speak with Ben.

"We are called to expose the truth," his attorney advised. "Sometimes its wiser to control the narrative. Would you be willing to grant just one interview?"

"That sounds better." *Better than spending the rest of my life fielding questions from reporters.* "Who would you suggest?"

"Tucker Carlson—he called yesterday." D.C. Dan asserted.

Discussing it over with Sara, she gave great encouragement.

"It might cost my job at the University," he relented.

"A small price to pay for the truth," she held him tight. "Who knows? Maybe God will use this to help save some lives."

At bedtime, he simply prayed: *"Lord, help me to rely on You, when I am before men."*

The following evening, Ben went *LIVE, in an Exclusive Interview, with Tucker Carlson on FOX.* Gone were the days of the TV Studio interview, where one would fly to New York, D.C. or L.A., under the hot lights of the camera on set. For the Broadcast, Ben simply used their home office computer with *Zoom*, in a split screen mode.

From the start, Tucker's tone and smile put Ben at ease, "Dr. Strickland, will you please give us a brief overview of your recent testimony before Senator Rand's committee?" To which Ben quickly related details of the deadly toxins found in the shots.

"It's observable science. We're the guys who look into a high-powered microscope to see what is really there," Ben tried sounding conversational, as his attorney suggested. "The inventor, Nicola Tesla, once said that science had become far too theoretical and numbers based. Formulaic. Take these so-called 'vaccines.' It doesn't take a rocket scientist to see that more people come down with the SARS-Covid virus, *after* a shot or booster. We observed that *after* one of these injections, there is a proliferation of Covid-19 spike proteins. It permeates into the cells and organs."

"So, you are saying that people become sick from the shots?" Tucker asked knowingly.

"Or worse. Don't we all know someone who was healthy and then became ill, or even died, *after* taking one of these toxic shots?" Ben continued more confidently now, in his element. "The mRNA was designed to be gene-modifying from a CRISPR CAS9 gene-splicing process. It introduces a third encoded genetic strand, essentially altering our God-given DNA. It's irreversible." *Maybe this revealed too much...*

"Are we speaking about potential Transhumanism?" Tucker rotated his head slowly, side-to-side. "Horrifying! —Horrifying to consider the unknown consequences here." Then changing direction, Tucker asked, "You're a Christian, aren't you Dr. Strickland? A rare occurrence for a scientist, these days..."

Ben collected his thoughts, not expecting the question. A scripture came to mind, *'Trust that I will give you the words in the moment'...* "There are more of us than people realize," he finally answered. "Again, for many it's the observable science. I recently had one colleague come to believe in our Creator, after realizing that *Genesis is History*." Ben went on, oblivious to the multitudes watching on live TV.

"The flood account of Noah is real. An area such as the Grand Canyon was formed rather quickly—not over billions of years, as the Darwinists' say. And the *Big Bang*? Don't explosions cause destruction not creation? We observe order and beauty in nature. God designed the human genome for natural healing. Consider the hummingbird, or the eyes on peacock feathers. All creation groans of God. The Bible in the Gospel of John explains that Jesus was with God from the beginning and that *ALL* things were created through Him. And man is created in His image."

"Amen," Tucker nodded. Oh, one last thing Dr. Strickland. "What can you tell us about the Pentagon connection, contracts and payoffs with the manufacturers of these injections?"

"Let's ask—was this a Military operation? Why do they want everyone in the world to take these debilitating shots?

The Bible refers to *'Marking.'* My hope is that the Senator's, like Rand and Johnson, will continue to investigate further and look into the DARPA, HHS, NIH, connections."

"Deep State," Tucker interjected. "Investigators need to follow the money. And we hope that there are others willing to come forward like you. Thank you for your time, Dr. Strickland." And with that it was over.

An intern in the newsroom came on his screen and asked Ben how he thought it all went. "Are there any questions you have?"

"Please thank Tucker for me and see if y'all can find out about what happened to Dr. Cole and all the doctors or scientists who have disappeared, or died under dubious circumstances. Oh—and please have someone investigate the graphene oxide/pharma connection to 5G towers," he finished.

Opening the door of his home office, Sara and the dog both embraced him at once. "Good job sweetie! We watched it with the sound level down, so the delay would not disturb you. Jessica and I baked you a chocolate mayo cake!"

Working their way into the kitchen, he chuckled, "There's a piece missing." Marshal sat reclined in Ben's favorite chair. "I see you have a few crumbs at the corner of your mouth."

"Observable science," Marshal held a fork in his direction.

While getting ready for bed later, Sara's cell phone rang. It was her dad from the West Coast.

"Is Ben handy?" he asked. "I saw him on the TV just now."

"Well, it's late here dad, but thanks for calling." Ben nodded while brushing his teeth and she activated the phone speaker.

"That was quite an interview, Ben. Had no idea you have been so involved in all of this. I'm starting to realize these shots are not what they were purported to be."

"Thanks for calling, dad. You were the one who educated me that, *'A virus mutates too quickly for a vaccine to ever be effective and that five years of trials was the standard.'*"

"Yes, and I believe you are right. These are *not* vaccines by any stretch of the imagination—is there a way for someone inoculated with this mRNA to test for any issues?"

"We have heard antibody tests, or a *D-dimer test,* for clotting are given. There several protocols for detoxing from the spike proteins, when someone becomes ill."

"We'll email you some natural regimens," Sara added.

Switching gears, Ben encouraged, "How's that great golf swing going?"

"Still golfing my age, but its harder to get any distance."

Sara chimed in, "You taught me to swing like *'twisting in a barrel,'* and to keep my head down with eyes on the ball."

"Speaking of feeling a little down—have to admit I've not felt quite the same since taking that blasted Pfizer shot."

"Can I pray for you, dad?" Sara persisted:

"Dear Father God. We pray for my dad's health, and ask for wisdom and knowledge. We pray for anything not of You to be cast out, purified and washed clean by the healing, loving blood of Jesus. And thank you that he's still singing, Lord!"

At the end of the week, Marshal received a call from a friend at Macrosoft. He wanted to meet with Ben to discuss the *Mark of the Beast*.

"You met Jon at our wedding," Marshal reminded. "I've worked with him for many years and trust him even more now that he's a believer. Jon's new to Christianity, Uncle Ben, but really knows what's happening from the inside."

"When and where does he want to meet?"

"Said he will fly out from Bellevue and meet tonight, then fly us back home."

Under the cover of darkness, Jon would be meeting them on the runway of a private executive airport in Asheville.

Ben realized this younger fellow was a man of means, when the older pilot addressed him as "Sir," stepping off the Falcon.

After discussing the book of Revelation, *the Mark* and their own personal faith, Jon changed the subject, "Look, we hope that people who got the shots, may have received a placebo, or one of the injections not containing the RNA/DNA changing properties. Only God knows for sure. He's the final judge, right?"

"Yes," Ben agreed.

"I really appreciate everything you have been doing to get the word out about the plans of the global elite." Jon reached out to shake his hand, while boarding the stairway to the Leer Jet. Reaching inside of his suitcoat, he handed Ben an envelope, "Please read this later," he said, "I wrote it one night after coming to the ultimate conclusion, it's a little rough—but I believe its true," Jon finished.

Ben thanked him and gave him one of the Little Bibles, "There's one verse from each of the books in the Bible."

Marshal and Jessica made ready to leave, giving Ben a hug and climbing the stairs to the Falcon. Marshal turned and waved saying, "Keep up the good fight Uncle Ben!"

Then, while walking the steps to his plane, Jon reached the top and spun around. Tapping on the side, he said, "Hey, let me know if you ever need to borrow this for a getaway," he offered. "You will understand more after reading the end of my letter."

Stopping at an all-night diner, Ben ripped the letter open. It was neatly typed on several smaller pages. He read:

Why is what they are calling a "vaccine" the 'Mark of the Beast?'

Why don't people 'get it' (that it's the MOTB?) It's because they've already taken it, or are deceived by the devil. Those who drink alcohol or already take drugs and pharmaceuticals are much more likely to take it.

—**Did it come by deception?**
In Revelation 18:23 it says, "And ALL Nations were deceived."

So, have all the nations been deceived? The answer is 'Yes!' All Nations were shut down until they agreed to push the shots.

—**The 'Scamdemic?'** The whole 'scamdemic' was for the vaccine, the vaccine was *not* for the scamdemic.

—**Has this ever happened before?** No, all nations were deceived...

—**Is it a 'Vaccine?'** Is it really a vaccine? Or is that part of the deception? No, it does not fit the definition of a traditional vaccine, they called it a vaccine to deceive.

—**What does it really do?** What did they say it won't do but actually does? It changes DNA doesn't it? At first, they boasted they found a way to change DNA. Then they said it doesn't change DNA, but it does...so no longer are you made in the image of God, you're in the image of the beast. It creates a triple helix, it adds in the extra chromosomes, with other lab DNA. You become a hybrid if you've taken it...don't you?

—**Did they tell you what was in it?** Did they tell you what was in this so-called vaccine? No—they didn't, did they?

—What was on the list of ingredients? All they included with the Vials was just a blank page. It was empty, wasn't it?

They didn't tell you there was Chimera and other animal cells, animal DNA, non-human DNA. They forgot to tell you this didn't they? They never mentioned the aborted baby fetal cells, no—the *murdered baby parts*. Did they tell you that you receive a MAC address and you become chipped with this so-called vaccine? How does one really know that they are chipped? It's simple. Download the Bluetooth app and go into public place with Wi-Fi and you will see your MAC address show up on the Bluetooth. MAC stands for *Media Access Control*. VaxXed people show up on Bluetooth. Why would someone show up on Bluetooth if it's only a vaccine? That's because you're tracked. Deception. These contain self-assembling nanotech. Nanobots assemble once inside the body. So when you're in a crowd, are vaxxed people shedding, or emitting dangerous EMF, electromagnetic radiation, among other things? We need to be more concerned about being in close proximity to the ones who have taken the shots, not the other way around!

—**Is it safe and effective?** Is it doing what they say it will do? Does it prevent disease? No, no, not at all, there is no benefit, none whatsoever. Zero. Ask yourself why are they pushing this so hard if there's no benefit whatsoever? There's a benefit to them, but there's not a benefit to those who take it. What does it really do? Clots. It gives blood clots. Or is this the self-assembling graphene oxide and Spike protein proliferating throughout the body?—-So, it's definitely not safe and effective since definitely not a vaccine. A vaccine would not have a MAC address and self-assembling technology. A real vaccine will not change your DNA. It would not have been brought about by deception, because they would not have had to deceive anyone if it was really a safe vaccine.

—Does it have the name of the beast in it?
Luciferase... yes it does. It stands for: '*Lucifer's Race*'

They call it "Luciferase," it is Bio luminescent. In Revelation 13, it says "Or the name of the Beast and that no man may buy or sell, save that they had the Mark for those who take it. So with *Luciferous* you are marked. You appear under the purple luminescent lights, or in airport scanners. The people that take it can easily show up everywhere. That's why they're installing all these purple lights around the world; so they can see the bioluminescence in a person. It's *marking you*, tracking you wherever you go. Luciferase? It's real, look it up...it's named after the Beast. Ask why the phony nose test is shoved in so far? What's really on it? Are they mocking us? The answer is, "Yes."

— And Rev. 13 also says, "Or the Number of his name." And his number is 600 threescore and six. Or 666.

So, there is a patent ending in 060606. Were they trying to deceive with this? When you remove the zeros, as we do with computer coding, it is 666.

—And the name? The name is really 'Lucifers Race,' isn't it? Are those who took it now part of 'Lucifer's Race,' instead of one of God's children made In His Image? Do the people that take it become part of Lucifer's race? Many of these jabs literally change the DNA.

—Why would a vaccine have so many materials in it that do not belong in the human body? Graphene Oxide doesn't belong in the human body. Why are people being magnetized? Why can someone stick a key to their skin and it stays in place? It's because they are magnetized. Why? It's about being on the grid.

It was brought about by deception, they deceived All Nations, they lied naming it a vaccine, it changes DNA, it creates a triple helix, it has all manner of toxic material in it that doesn't belong there, satanic sorcery, murdered baby fetal parts, Chimera and animal DNA, parasites, nanotechnology, graphene oxide, and it has Luciferase, a bioluminescence that Marks and tracks someone. Telling us it is "Lucifers Race".

And the nanotechnology, graphene oxide and metals in the shots? What were these for? 5G. Ask yourself, why were they installing 5G when everyone was locked down? It serves as a transmitter and a receiver. The ones who took the so-called vaccines, can be controlled by an outside source. Nanotechnology, the MAC address, creating people to become an operating system, why? Because people will need to take this DNA altering shot to buy and sell. That is clear in the Book of Revelation as part of the mark of the beast. So, it can go from what they're calling a vaccine—to *The Mark*. The vaccine passport within someone is a digital ID, now being set up for a person to be allowed to buy and sell. It is critical for the global elitists to make sure your DNA is changed, before they will allow you to buy and sell. But a believer in Jesus has God's true Mark.

These are not vaccines; were they planned to 'Mark' a person? Not to mention, that these shots are also killing people all over the world. The digital ID, or vaccine passport, outside the body, will not damn a person, but it is the devil's DNA altering snakebite, needed to buy and sell, that can damn a person."

The letter ended but there was a handwritten note with several Bible verses at the bottom.

Dear Uncle Ben, (I hope you don't mind me calling you that). Thank you for being such a truth telling believer in these times. Because of you sharing your faith with Marshal, I am now a "Born again Believer," in Jesus Christ. He's the Lord and leader of my life. A time is coming when we may not be able to communicate like this, and I wanted to thank you personally, and to get your input on my letter. Above is my personal contact information.

ONE MORE ITEM SO IMPORTANT:

I fear you may want to consider disappearing for a while, after your Senate testimony. Let's just say that I overheard some things about silencing the opposition. If it comes to it, please contact me, or Marshal and we will do everything possible to help. Other than that, May God bless the remnant! Jon

Here are a few verses that go along with my letter:

"The devil came to steal, kill and destroy and to 'Mark' with his number, and his name, and his DNA. But "Jesus came to give life and life in abundance."

"And they are tormented day and night, whosoever receiveth the 'Mark' of his name." Rev. 14:11

"And men were scorched with great heat and blasphemed the name of God, which have power over these plagues and they repented not to give him glory. And the fifth angel poured out his vial upon the seat of the beast and his kingdom was full of darkness and they gnawed their tongues for pain. And blaspheme the God of Heaven, because of their pains and their sores and repented not of their deeds." Rev. 16:9-11

The following morning, Ben wrote a quick response to Jon;

Your letter aligned with my convictions on this MOB/VaX. We are living "As in the days of Noah," when the demons came into the daughters of men, changing their DNA, creating a race of evil giants and their wicked offspring, and God sent the flood (Genesis 6). There were only eight people who got on the Ark. Once again, with the devil's DNA, we're in the days of Noah, as Jesus says in the Book of Matthew. Prepare for the floodgates to open. Bless you for the meeting and the heads-up for our safety, with an offer to help—we will pray about it. Trusting In Jesus and the Great commission, Ben

Here's one scripture that helped open our eyes:

"And the light of a candle shall shine no more at all in thee; and the voice of the bridegroom and of the bride shall be heard no more at all in thee: for thy merchants were the great men of the earth; for by thy sorceries (pharmakeia) were ALL Nations deceived." Revelation 18:23

Chapter 13
"COME OUT OF HER MY PEOPLE"

The following *day of rest* was spent with Ben and Sara

spending time in prayer, fasting, and reading scripture. Together they sought direction from God.

Studying Revelation and Matthew 24, Ben shared, "Some will be martyred or even beheaded, for their love of Christ. But a remnant, will be hidden from God's Wrath."

Searching her notes, she replied, "In Revelation, 18:8 it says, *'the merchants of the earth will be thrown down in one day. And those who worship the Beast will cry and mourn when it is made desolate.'*"

"Merchants of *Pharmakeia*! In Matthew 24: Jesus says, 'flee to the mountains!'" Ben interjected with fervor.

Undaunted, Sara went on, "This is Babylon, the *'City of Commerce'* that became rich by the Sorcery of Pharmakeia; Pharmaceuticals,"

"Has to be New York City. Or *ALL* of the country."

She continued, *"Therefore shall her plagues come in one day, death and mourning and famine; utterly burned in fire; for strong is the Lord God who judgeth her..."*

"Maybe its time we consider moving to a remote missionary field." She knew when his tone was serious.

"Well, if we're going to be leaving, what would we do with dear Kimmy?"

"I'm sure Miriam would love a well-trained guard dog and best friend until we get our bearings," he ended. On cue, a tear formed in the corner of her eye. Lamenting not only for her faithful pet; thoughts of leaving family, friends and her beloved preschoolers, pricked her heart, as well.

Bright and early, a call came in from Pastor A.J., "Thanks for sending me your synopsis on the altering of God's seeds.

We added it to the church site and it created quite a stir.

At tomorrow's service my own discovery may surprise you!"

Ben's synopsis read:

Many people worldwide have taken the mRNA, or other Protein Adjuvant injections, believing they were helping themselves, or others. Many took what they labeled a 'vaccination' due to government and media manipulation. Many lined up for the shots, out of fear. As a Genetic Lab Researcher, and Christ follower, we found these 'inoculations,' will rather cause illness, or even death to oneself or others.

If you haven't taken any shots, don't take them. NONE—not one! If you have taken any of them, PLEASE do not take any further shots. The call is to 'Repent for trusting in man and medicine over God.' Beg Him for healing with forgiveness. Remember the Lord has mercy with our repentance. Lamentations says: 'They are new every morning, great is thy faithfulness.'

Now these mRNA and Adjuvant 'Jabs' have the ability to go break through a nucleus and reverse transcribe DNA into your cells. They are creating CDNA, complementary DNA, which can be owned and patentable by pharmaceutical companies. The mRNA carries instructions, a payload, and adds an additional 72,000 genome to a person's DNA, a Triple Helix.

When we studied all of these structures under an electron microscope, we discovered the Vials contained graphene Nano ribbons, the Darpahydrogels, the self-assembling Nano chips, Parasites and Luciferase, for marking and tracking.

THE FINAL SEED

All of these same structures are now being found in literally every kind of injectable imaginable; Flu shots, polio, measles, all of them. They are creating human hybrids with parasites and animal DNA. We are in the days of Noah, as Jesus said.

The Bible says we are to 'Come out of her, my people,' and set ourselves apart as believers. Plead the blood of Jesus for God to save in these perilous days.

Jesus come quickly: Maranatha!

Brother, Ben Strickland

At *the Little White Church*, in the morning, the video screen carried a compelling message:

DNA is a Sacred active Blueprint of God
Don't let Demonic Forces Alter Yours!

After several songs of Worship and Praise, Pastor A.J. called Ben and Sara forward. "Many of you have come to know and love this special couple over their brief time here."

A.J. laid hands on each of their shoulders. "We have some exciting news! Ben and Sara have been called to the mission field; Ben will be assisting with health care instruction and Sara teaching English to the village children."

"Sharing the Gospel message too, of course" Ben piped in.

Calling others forward, the leaders took turns giving heartfelt 'Sending Prayers' for their new Missionary life.

"May you both move mountains in the 'Montaña's of Centro America!'" The worship leader encouraged.

During the message, Pastor A.J. preached methodically, "I have learned quite a bit about DNA from Ben—Dr. Strickland.

"We have discussed both the scientific and spiritual ramifications of all that is unraveling now. God's Holy name sheds even more light on this. Try and hang with me;" A.J. directed everyone's attention to the large screen.

"The DNA genome is a right-sided helix made up of Adenine, Thymine, Cytosine and Guanine. The helix is held together by sulfuric bonds, that appear after every ten pairs of nucleotides." A.J. looked up from his notes, "How my doing so far, Dr. Strickland?"

"Great Pastor! Just call me Ben—we're all with you..."

A.J. preached on, pointing up to the display on the large Video screen: "It comes to every 5 pair, every 6 pair and every 5 pair of nucleotides. That's 10 – 5- 6 – 5, or in the Hebrew Alphabet (Aleph Bet) YOD HE VAV HE, or YAHWEH.

The Holy name of God in the Bible."

The video screen showed: Y - H - V - H

10 5 6 5

"It's the signature of God, our Creator. It's on every cell. He's signing His painting, if you will...Now this Messenger RNA, is adding another strand of DNA with the injections. In Hebrew, the third strand changes the name. In Hebrew it becomes: 10 – 5 – 6 – 5 -/ 6 – 6 – 6. The third strand corresponds in Hebrew to 666! Or as it says in Revelation, *Six Hundred Three Score and Six.* 6 times 60 times 600 is: 216,000. When you add both sides and another 72,000, it totals 216,000. --not bad for a guy that got C's in Math." The corners of A.J.'s mouth curled upward under the thick beard.

Reaching for a glass of water, he simultaneously lifted the old KJV Bible, steadying himself under its weight.

"What does this all this mean then? Let me read a scripture: *'Let him who has understanding calculate the number of the Beast...for it is the number of a man; and his number is six hundred, three score and six.'* It's the Devils name. But *Gods'* Holy name—Y H V H—is written on those made in His image. And the *Devils' Marks* are written *'IN'* those he takes with him into the pit." A.J. gazed heavenward.

"In Revelation 7:3, an angel declares, *'Hurt not the earth until we have sealed the servants of God in their foreheads.'*"

Departing from handwritten notes he asked, "Are you sealed by God with His Holy Mark?" He began moving mightily in the power of the Holy Spirit:

"Listen, we have to be careful as believers here. Its not for us to condemn. At the end of the day, we hope those friends, family and brothers taking the devils poison, had a placebo. Rare, most likely. Possibly, they took just one and it was not mRNA, and DNA altering, with the *Luciferase*, or ability to *Mark* them. Let's face it, the odds go down exponentially, with more than one shot. At the same time, how many people prayed to the Lord and consulted scripture before taking these toxins?

"Scripture says, *'We each work out our own Salvation with fear and trembling and we see through the glass dimly now.'* Well, I'm trembling right now in the sight of a Holy, Righteous and Almighty God, and I'm not taking one. Many of you know I'm a former Green Beret. We were trained to take the bullet for one another. But not take the Mark of the Beast. Is this a hill to die on?"

A.J. studied their sullen faces now riveted on every word. Quoting from Joshua he answered his own question, *"For me and my house, we shall serve the Lord.'* For me it is..."

Suddenly, the little old pink hat lady stood up declaring: "Friends! If you don't see it as *the Mark of the Beast*, eventually you will take it!" The room sat silent. Stunned.

Winding up the sermon, A.J. asked the question on everyone's mind, **"Is it repentable?"** The words bellowed, hanging alone in the humid summer air—"Revelation goes on to say, *'And the light of the candle shall shine no more in them.'"* Gazing heavenward again, he finished, "May God have mercy – May God have mercy on us all."

On the very next morning at work, Ben was fired. It seemed Dr. Pidgeon took delight in calling him into the office, "Tough luck, Ben. And next month you were eligible for tenure." The only reason given, "Cutbacks."

Charlie promised to find them another position, however, Ben knew the Lord was saying, *"Come out of her, my people!"*

The following week was spent preparing. It seemed daunting to pack up one's whole life in a suitcase, or two. It was less burdensome, however, to consider leaving to higher ground, as tragic scenes around the country and the world poured in; with economic collapse, riots, mass murders, 'wars and rumors of war.' This time nuclear.

THE FINAL SEED

A catastrophic tsunami here, or earthquake there came daily now. An eight-point event on the Richter Scale, rocked from Turkey through to the Golan Heights in Israel, sadly killing thousands. And a level 4 hurricane currently pounded off their own Coast. Thankful, to ride it out in the Carolina mountains, but high-wind advisories for falling trees and even tornadoes were given.

None of the top scientists Ben knew, believed a lick about so-called *Climate Change*. He knew man often messed with God's weather under *The Firmament*, yet he also knew that judgment from the throne of God prevailed. '*Noah knew all about climate change*,' Ben would say at the men's group.

Maybe I'm stress eating, Sara herself ruminated one morning, *my waist feels a little thick and all my dresses seem tight. Am I being selfish? Right now, one of Ben's cousins is in a quarantine camp in Canada. Shot free, though.*

Trepidation turned to joy, when their home sold quickly. The day after signing a sales contract, the Dean of his University called Ben directly, offering his job back with a raise. "Dr. Pidgeon is on hiatus. Between us, it was discovered he received unauthorized payments from various drug companies."

Ben politely declined the offer, saying he was hopeful for the Lab and would stay in touch. A Mission called.

Sara recalled the innocent children and family-oriented people she came to embrace on her own prior mission trips. *The children were always so dear everywhere in the world. Hopefully, they would send for Kimmy, or family may visit. Jesus' words echoed in her mind now, "Everyone who leaves houses, family or friends, or country for my namesake...will inherit everlasting life..."*

Ben had promised, 'first things first!' *They would plant an organic garden on their Hectare of land in the mountains of Centro America. The home not as important to her. She imagined a Casa, with peeling paint and weeds poking through cracked cement floors.*

Early in the morning, Charlie and their neighbor, Miriam, drove them to the GSP Airport. Sara laid her head on Ben's lap, in the backseat, *an hour and a half to Greenville, sans traffic.* On the drive, Charlie was encouraged to stick with the Lab and publish their combined work.

Helping with their bags from the SUV, Charlie said, "We want to visit you, Ben!" There was a group hug, a sending prayer and a few tears.

Walking into the terminal Ben mentioned, "Did you notice they were holding hands?"

"And Charlie opened her car door and said 'we,'" Sara smiled, while rolling her bags towards the ticket counter.

Boarding the plane, Sara's prayer departed from flight safety for the Capitan, *although many had heart issues, or close calls now while in the air,* due to the mandated shots. Instead, her prayer was both broader and specific.

In the aisleway, she whispered, "Dear Lord, *'Bless us indeed, expand our territory, keep Your hand upon us and keep the evil one away!'*

Lifting their bags in the overhead, Ben added, "And Lord, help us get all of these organic seeds through customs."

Reclining back in the seat brought a sigh of relief. Ben had considered calling Jon, who had offered them his private jet, *the falcon.* But pretension was a consideration where they were headed, and he hoped to blend in now.

Ben had researched a mission field open to the Gospel, free from any mandates. *No masks, no tests, no shots.* The Spanish speaking pastor had even said, *"Ni siquiera las mascaras que apestan."*

Sara translated, "They are never wearing any masks, and masks *stink,*" she laughed.

"It's a completely independent remnant group, like *The Little White Church*, where Pastors don't even take a salary."

"A.J. believes we are headed for the *'organic, underground church,'* like in the book of Acts," she recalled.

Now on the 737, Ben recalled all they had been through in the last couple of years. *The angel in the book of Daniel said things would increase, moving faster, in the end days. Only possible through technology, most likely,* he considered.

First saying silent prayers, for those he knew dying or maimed from the *Bio Weapon, the shots,* or *hospital protocols. The ones exposing the evils who mysteriously disappeared. Faithful names, like Marcus Lamb, Russ Dizdar, Rob Skiba, or Dr. Zelenko—from the convention, all were gone. The CDC site's VAERS Reports showed a million more.*

So many of those who Died Suddenly at younger ages, included sports stars, famous actors, newscasters, writers, or military and first responders. Ben even knew of three Russian doctors that mysteriously fell from hospital windows.

Not many, such as Stew Peters, or Robert F. Kennedy Jr., were going strong, after exposing the truth about the injections.

"A penny for your thoughts," Sara held his hand tightly, as they rolled left, after liftoff.

"Better make it in *Colones*—our new currency."

She felt drained, exhausted from the recent events of the day. Their rushed move. Something else was affecting her physically, but she was reluctant to fully consider, or share. Her heart was full, though, knowing the Lord was directing their steps. "There's something I need to tell you, Ben."

"What is it, sweetie?"

"It never seemed an appropriate time—and now in flight?"

"We're leveling off," he reassured. "I'd love to know..."

"Umm—its been over three months since my last period."

"What?" he swallowed the word.

"You know—I know it sounds like a miracle at my age, but I think we might be having a baby..."

The plane gently rocked from side-to-side, as Ben embraced the news. Closing his eyes momentarily, his long fingers caressed her hand. *Dear Lord*, he prayed, *could this be true?* Then in a *still small voice,* came a sweet answer. Gently, his hand slipped down onto her belly now.

"Let's have this baby at home, then. Let's have this baby at our new home."

Chapter 14
Post Script

Rising above a thick layer of clouds, their aircraft reached a cruising altitude in a matter of minutes. High on an easy southern wind now, they would be over the Capitol of Georgia. Far below them, in front of the Centers for Disease Control, in Atlanta, stood a tall street preacher holding a sign; long dark hair and matted beard. Several passers-by strained to decipher the prophetic words coming briskly in a thick Georgia drawl:

"I will treat it as if it *is the Mark*—me and my family will never get it! We all know people who got it, or loved ones have. A lot of them have already died. If it *is* the Mark, what

Bible verse says there is salvation for anyone getting the Mark?! It has *LucifeRACE* in it. *No jab—no job?* If it changes the DNA, its got to be the Mark! How much more obvious must it be that people should *NOT* get it?! People didn't stop at one. They KEPT getting them. They're still drinking the Kool-Aid! They gave them to their children, as if they belong to a Jim Jones's cult.

"Jesus Himself says, 'Let him who reads understand.' For the innocent, we pray for God's mercy. My heart doesn't want to stop believing for miracles and healing."

The preacher lifted his megaphone, "At some point God says, *"Let the wicked keep on being wicked. Let the righteous keep on being righteous."* We're called to *warn, pray* and *share God's Word*. To be a '*Watchman on the Wall*'. If people don't listen, we dust off our feet and move on. Three years ago, I sent all of my relatives and friends a warning video on the shots; *BEFORE* it was released. Dr. Carrie Madej is from here in Georgia. If it's the Mark, I told my sphere of influence. I'm still warning. When people don't listen, the blood is on their own head. It says in Ezekiel 3 that our *'conscience is clean'.*

"Right in this state, the Georgia Guidestones, called for depopulating the earth to half a billion people. Now they blow them up! Mysteriously gone, like they never existed.

We have to be ready. The *'Pre-Tribbers'* say they won't have to go through Tribulation. But in Matthew 24, Jesus says He comes at the *'Last Trumpet.'* In John 6, Jesus says four times He will raise up *EVERYONE* the Father has given him, *At the LAST day!* It says, *'He who endures to the end shall be saved!'*

"Maybe it's the plague that kills one-third of the earth's population. It's prophesied in Revelation. Did you hear our government purchased over 7,000 guillotines? The Bible says: *'Those who lose their life for Jesus's sake will find it and they will receive a martyr's reward.'* God is merciful. Not wanting any to perish, but for all to come to repentance. Maybe we're *in* the tribulation now! Things are not always what people interpret. Many times, they are not! We're all looking for the 3rd temple to be built in Jerusalem on Mt. Moriah; "BUT WE ARE THE TEMPLE MADE WITHOUT HANDS!"

It very well could be the *'Abomination of Desolation,'* spoken of by Daniel the Prophet, because **We are the temple of the Holy Spirit!** It says in Daniel that the Clay and the Iron cannot be mixed. God did not mix iron technology into our bodies, but He molded us out of the clay. So if mankind willingly alters the DNA and merges with machine, then a person is no longer a creation of God. Transhumanism, nanotechnology, gene therapy, and cybernetic implants will be the end of humanity. So-called 'Artificial Intelligence' is filled with demons! The generation that sees these things, starting with the abomination of desolation will surely not pass away until the gathering of His people from the four corners of earth be fulfilled. It's happening quickly. If it's the abomination, we just witnessed the GREAT FALLING AWAY. FOR SURE! THE TIME IS NEAR!"

The Preacher continued, asking the small crowd: "What if the seven-year tribulation began with the Covid shenanigans and the Abraham peace agreements? The whole world has never seen anything like this. When they shall say, 'Peace and Safety,' then sudden destruction comes. Noahide Laws and the Red Horseman of Revelation are soon here! The CDC mocks you with a Zombie Apocalypse! Its on their site." Several cars sped by honking their horns.

"God wanted people to REPENT before the flood of Noah. Many knew about God, but refused to get on the Ark. They died. Why are so-called righteous people dying? THE END IS NEAR!

"So many Christians believe there's no way the Jab could be the Mark. They say we'll KNOW it is, before we get it. Really? Is Satan obvious, or is he sneaky? How long did it take for Adam and Eve to sin in the garden? *How long does it take to eat forbidden fruit? About the same amount of time it takes to roll up one's sleeve!*"

The tall man took a deep breath, pacing the CDC sidewalk, "It's like the Ten Virgins in the Bible..."–Suddenly, a petite younger black woman touched his shoulder. The preacher spun around, almost knocking her down with his sign.

"I know Yeshua," the younger lady smiled. "Jesus died for my sin on the cross and conquered death."

"Hallelujah!" the preacher responded.

Pointing up at the large CDC signs, fronting the twin buildings, she blurted, "They fired me two years ago. I refused their shots. They *do* use aborted fetal cells. I knew it was from the devil." Her lips began to quiver, "You mentioned The Virgins in the Bible. The ones keeping their oil trimmed, that's me—don't want my babies tainted."

"Praise God!" the preacher smiled for the first time that day. "Well then make sure you marry an *Unmarked Man*."

"Will do!" she lifted her eyes, hastily running to board a bus. Waving back, she called out, "God bless! God bless you, preacher man!"

He fired back up on the quest: "One more thing. Don't be fooled by the demons. True Bible scholars see UFO activity as demonic. The demons have been masquerading as extraterrestrials since the beginning. They will say aliens are invading but in reality, they're demonic fallen angels. Space agencies are fake. We're not on a round speck of dust in the middle of nowhere! The Bible says there's a Heaven above, a Hell below and a beautiful blue firmament dome covering.

"The next step of the beast system is digital money and the Micro Needle Patches. *No 'stick or prick' or nano-ID—no buying or selling*. People worry about work, bank failures or CERN. More importantly fear God! Worry about being sealed by God. You either belong to God or the devil."

As dark clouds began forming above, he begged: "If you've been deceived, plead the blood of Jesus to save you! He's coming soon on clouds of Glory!"

Lifting his worn sign again, he swiveled to face the tall windows of the CDC building. Several workers inside peered down at the scene on the street below. Slowly, his hand raised towards the building, while reciting a final scripture: *"Be not deceived; God is not mocked: for whatsoever a man soweth, that he also reaps!"*

Turning to leave, he swelled up with one last word of sage advice: *"Repent!* For the Axe is at the root of the tree!"

Dedication

This Book is dedicated to Jesus Christ; written in forty days. I heard, *"Chronicle the times and the seasons when the seed of man again became corrupted."* This story, with its many parallels to our own lives, is also dedicated to my devoted wife, who trusts in the Lord with all of her heart. She is well acquainted with endurance...

Heartfelt Disclaimer:
Our greatest resource of all is the *Greatest Physician of All*—our God and Creator. May this encourage you to trust first in the Lord for healing, provision and protection. We are called to take responsibility for our *Temple of God*, staying whole in the way it was designed. Turning solely to God and His Word for discernment. Where do we find all the answers? They are *ALL* found in His Holy Word.

"That he might present it to Himself a glorious church, not having spot, or wrinkle, or any such thing; but that it should be holy and without blemish."* Ephesians 5:27, KJV

Acknowledgments:

With deep love and gratitude for editing and holy input, by my amazing wife, Elizabeth Soldahl. Much appreciation to so many folks who directly or indirectly inspired me to write this Novel: The 'Watchmen on the Wall.' Parents, Sons, Daughters, Family, Friends and Faithful Ministers.

Contact information:
ericsoldahl@gmail.com
Website: www.faithonfire.net[1]

*Names are fictitious or changed for privacy and protection.
*Scripture taken from the Holy Bible, KJV, NKJV.
*Note: The Author and Publisher take no responsibility for the health or actions of others. The information therein is not meant to replace medical advice, either directly or indirectly. This is a work of Fiction, from a Historical and Biblical perspective.

THE FINAL SEED

Fiction/Novel/Christian/Inspirational

"HE WHO ENDURES TO THE END SHALL BE SAVED"

What Readers are Saying:

"Loved how the author brought you into close relationship with the characters like you were part of their small awake community. Highly recommend this book for ALL to read!" Maede B.

"A Holy Spirit filled download! For all of you 'Covid Conspiracy Naysayers,' this is a game-changer. James D.

"Those who read this book will have no excuse on judgement day, because they will have been warned." Julia K.

"One of the best books I have read. I couldn't put it down, important message for everyone. A must read. 5 Stars." Anne M.

"The shots will never be viewed in the same way. This Novel is a must for anyone considering 'The Mark.' Filled with faith and facts.

The devil is in the details..." David H.

Printed in the USA
CPSIA information can be obtained
at www.ICGtesting.com
CBHW021125240324
5780CB00010B/685

9 781735 625423